HORSES OF

HALF MOON
RANCH

SKYLARK

D1375378

SKYLARK

JENNY OLDFIELD

Illustrated by
Paul Hunt

Hodder
Children's
Books

a division of Hodder Headline Limited

With thanks to Bob, Karen and Katie Foster, and to the staff and
guests at Lost Valley Ranch, Deckers, Colorado

First published in Great Britain in 2001
by Hodder Children's Books

A Catalogue record for this book is available from the British Library

ISBN 0 340 79173 X

Typeset by Avon Dataset Ltd, Bidford-on-Avon, Warks

Printed and bound in Great Britain by
The Guernsey Press Co. Ltd, Channel Isles

Hodder Children's Books
a division of Hodder Headline Limited
338 Euston Road
London NW1 3BH

1

'Whadya reckon?' Karina Cooper invited Kirstie Scott to comment on the latest arrival at Half-Moon Ranch.

Kirstie had answered the wrangler's call and emerged from the tack-room into the bright spring daylight. Now she stood squinting into the sun, trying to make out exactly what was going on in the arena.

Something was kicking up the dirt. It was bucking and charging the fences, showing all the signs of an animal who was definitely not happy to be there. The angry creature was the size of a six-week foal, yet not quite the right shape – head too big, ears too long. 'Hmm.' Kirstie climbed the high fence and perched on the top rail.

'Well?' Karina urged. There was a broad grin on her tanned face. 'Is she gonna make a kiddie-ride, or not?'

'What is it?' Kirstie pulled down the brim of her stetson so that it shaded her eyes from the sun. Through the dust and grit she saw the small creature grind to a halt, then raise its clumsy head and let out an ear-splitting cry.

Karina covered her ears. 'Meet Columbine,' she told Kirstie. 'And I wanna make it clear that she was not – repeat NOT – my idea!'

Eeee-aaaw! Eeee-aaw! The little lady in the arena had a big head, big ears and big, BIG voice.

'Jeez, it's a burro!' Kirstie breathed.

'You got it!' Karina laughed. 'Six months old and not enjoying being away from her momma.'

'Awww!' Kirstie's soft heart melted as the dusty little burro trotted into the shadow cast by the long, wooden tack-room. For the first time she got a clear view.

Eeee-awww! Columbine cried again.

The young donkey was grey and hairy, her back

marked with a thin dark cross. Her legs were skinny, her hooves tiny, but her ears and eyes were gigantic.

'Awww!'

'Already you sound like her!' Karina teased, pulling Kirstie down into the arena to take a closer look. 'How come I knew you were the kind of girl who would want to take care of a poor lone burro?'

'Who is she? Why is she here?' Kirstie asked.

Columbine had registered their approach. She tensed and got ready to buck her way out of a corner.

Karina paused, thumbs hooked through the belt loops of her jeans. Then she cocked her head towards the lean figure opening the gate and walking stiffly towards them. 'Don't ask me,' she teased. 'Ask Hadley here why we took in an ornery little burro when we already got our hands full taking care of the broodmares and their spring foals!'

'Columbine's part of the training programme I've got lined up for Moondance,' the old man explained at last.

Kirstie had hassled Hadley all morning. Getting

him to give reasons was like drawing blood out of a stone. He went around with his mouth clamped shut, first dragging a plastic manger into the arena and filling it with alfalfa then setting up a water supply for the burro. He'd got close enough to fasten a foal's halter round her head and had even given the thick, dusty coat a brush. By noon that Sunday in May, Columbine was settled down and eating quietly in her new home.

'How come?' Kirstie couldn't figure out his answer. 'How does a burro help you to train a four-year-old mare?'

'I'll show you,' he grunted, leading the way out to Red Fox Meadow to cut his beloved blue roan out from the ramuda and lead her back to the arena.

Moondance came eagerly with her high-stepping, rangy walk. She held her head up, with ears pricked, sensing something unusual on today's menu of events. But when Hadley took her into the arena and introduced her to Columbine, she snorted and held back.

'This here is your new buddy,' Hadley told the disgruntled mare, leading her to the shadowy corner where the burro had retreated. 'Sure, she ain't much to look at, with that big ugly head and those pointy ears, but I want you to give her a welcome and be real nice.'

Kirstie watched Moondance grow used to the idea of being in the arena with the odd-looking little burro. The beautiful mare's flattened ears gradually relaxed and she reached out her head in a faint gesture of curiosity.

Columbine still huddled in the corner, big eyes gleaming, spindly legs trembling.

Moondance took a step towards her. *Oh come on, scaredy-cat, I'm not gonna hurt you!*

The donkey pranced and skittered. Then she calmed down and let Moondance approach.

The sleek blue roan came close. She lowered her head and pushed her long nose with its flaring nostrils at Columbine's chunky, hairy face. Then she sniffed her way round the newcomer, as if to say: *What kind of pony are you, with that black cross on your back and hair sprouting out of your ears?*

Kirstie grinned. The pair looked like a cartoon duo: one tall, slim and elegant with flowing mane and tail; the other seeming like a clumsy copy of the original. *Poor Columbine!* she thought. Donkeys sure were short-changed in the good-looks department.

5

Eee-aw! The burro chose her own way to return Moondance's greeting. Breath sucked in on the *Eeee*; raucous, rasping out-breath on the *awww!*

The mare took a quick step back.

Even Hadley laughed at the shocked look on Moondance's face. 'Yeah, not exactly musical neither,' he commented, striding off and leaving the pair to get to know each other.

Kirstie ran after the old wrangler, still bursting with questions. 'So where does the burro fit in? I don't get it.'

'The burro will teach Moondance a whole lot,' he insisted. 'Stuff like sharing feed out of the manger, taking responsibility for another crittur. See, Moondance don't have the right herd mentality because of the way she was treated at Ty Turner's place.'

Kirstie nodded. The blue roan's previous owner had tried brutal methods to break her. She knew that Hadley favoured gentling over sacking out and cutting a horse's flesh with whips and ropes. 'Yeah, I get it. I know that Moondance had a bad start and she's nowhere near ready to join the dude string. And you're saying being in the company of the burro will help?'

6

'Sure.' Hadley stopped on the footbridge out to the meadow. The clear creek sparkled beaneath the wooden boards. The banks were lined with the bell-shaped spring flowers which the frightened little burro had been named after.

'Y'see, a burro ain't no threat to Moondance, not like some of the other horses in the ramuda. So Columbine makes a great companion, teaches the mare to look out for another, so she gets more of the herd mentality we need here on the ranch.'

'Neat!' Kirstie got the point. 'This way, we stop Moondance from being a bunch-quitter! She gets the idea of sticking with the other horses and not roaming off on her own.'

'Right.' Hadley nodded. He looked up at the midday sun, then at the horizon of pine-clad mountains. 'And now, if you don't mind, I've got a hundred chores to get through.'

'Neat!' Kirstie said again, after lunch. She was feeling upbeat, riding out on Five Mile Creek Trail with Karina and a bunch of new guests. 'Trust Hadley to come up with a novel way of schooling his mare!'

Karina grinned. She too was on a high, since Hadley had eventually seen fit to entrust

Moondance to her for the afternoon.

'Go easy on her mouth,' he'd instructed as she'd fitted the blue roan's bridle. 'I don't want you turning her bit-sour.'

Karina had raised one eyebrow. 'Hey Hadley, either you let me do this my way or else you ride your own horse, OK?'

But the old man had already acknowledged that no way would his novice mare make it up to Eden Lake with the advanced group. This was the toughest trail of all, and Moondance wasn't yet ready to ride with the 'grown-ups'. 'OK, OK,' he'd conceded. 'But just remember, Moondance don't like to lead. Put Kirstie up front on Lucky.'

Karina's other eyebrow had shot up.

Kirstie had muscled in fast. 'Let's go!' she'd hissed at Karina.

She and Lucky had led the intermediates out of the corral before Hadley had time to change his mind. It was only after Karina had cooled down that Kirstie had managed to explain the reason for the burro in the arena.

'You gotta hand it to Hadley,' Karina said grudgingly. 'No one knows more about horses than he does.'

'I'll tell him you said that,' Kirstie threatened, guiding her eight riders along a rocky track overlooking a thirty-foot drop into the rushing creek below.

'No way!' Karina held Moondance back to allow the ranch guests to pass. 'Hadley's head is way too big for his stetson already!'

'This sure is pretty!' The rider who was first in line behind Kirstie and Lucky whistled his admiration at the view. 'Time for a picture – Kodak moment!'

As he stopped his bay gelding, Squeaky, and held up the line, a few other guests followed his example, including one guy on Silver Flash with an expensive, digital, state-of-the-art camera. He zoomed in on two mule deer, who stood watching the horse riders from the safety of the far bank, took his photograph then spent forever carefully zipping his camera back inside his leather horn-bag.

'Hey, Leon!' Karina called from the back of the line. 'Could we get a move on there? My horse is a little nervous with heights.'

The guest nodded, but didn't seem to speed up. Instead he messed with zippers, gloves and reins. 'How do I get my horse to go?' he yelled at Kirstie, who was already clear of the narrow ridge and waiting in the shade of an aspen stand.

She tried not to react. 'You click your tongue at her,' she told Leon. 'And you press your legs against her sides. Don't pull at the reins – that'll confuse her!'

'Gee, I thought he was supposed to be intermediate!' another guest muttered. 'How come he didn't put himself with beginners?'

'Because he's Leon Powell!' someone else whispered.

'You mean, Leon Powell the artist?' Word went round the small group.

'Yeah, he's the painter who does the wildlife scenes. Right now he's flavour of the month with all the big Hollywood stars who like to get involved with conservation issues. His paintings sell for hundreds of thousands of dollars!'

Kirstie listened in to the whispered conversation, watching Silver Flash's rider with new interest. Leon Powell was a small, dark-haired guy with a tidy moustache. His movements were precise to the point of fussiness and he wore clothes that were carefully co-ordinated – pale blue denim shirt with Wrangler jeans and a dark blue spotted kerchief knotted round his neck.

'Yeah, I guess a famous wildlife artist couldn't own up to never going horse-riding before,' the guest who had begun the conversation admitted. 'It wouldn't exactly be cool.'

'You ready yet?' Karina was still having trouble with Moondance. Hadley's mare skittered sideways on the ledge, almost losing her footing and sending a shower of stones rattling down the cliff.

Leon Powell frowned. He sat stiff in the saddle, holding the reins in a vice-like grip and giving poor Silver Flash a hard time as the horse tried to edge forward. 'Who let that grey mare loose on the trail?' he grumbled. 'It's not even fully trained!'

'Go on, Leon, keep movin'!' Karina called loudly. Famous artist or not, she gave it to him straight. 'If you don't like this route, we can always move you down to ride with the beginners!'

The comment didn't improve Leon's temper as he finally joined Kirstie and the others under the aspens. 'Since when did they employ female wranglers on dude ranches?' he muttered nastily. 'You take a guy – he always knows when to keep his mouth shut. But this gal could holler for America!'

Kirstie bit her tongue. Maybe now that he was

11

off the ledge, Leon Powell would quit grumbling and enjoy the ride. She turned to lead the group out on to a clear stretch of hillside, scattered with bright splashes of paint-brush cacti in flower and with the sharp green spikes of yuccas. But before they were clear of the trees, she heard Moondance spook and kick up a storm.

She turned to see Karina sit firm in the saddle as the blue roan bucked.

'What happened?' an anxious woman guest asked.

'A mule deer stepped out and spooked her!' Karina yelled, completely cool and in control. As Moondance bucked she drew the reins in tight; then as the horse rocked backwards she shifted her weight to lean forward in the saddle. One sharp jab with her silver spurs convinced her mount that it was time to calm down.

'Ouch!' The nervous woman winced.

'Yeah, is that really necessary?' Leon Powell wanted to know.

'It works, don't it?' came Karina's brusque reply. 'At a time like that, you gotta show who's in charge here.' As she joined the group, they saw that the short argument between horse and rider had brought Moondance out in a sweat across her withers and that her mouth bubbled with froth.

The uneasy silence told Kirstie that the artist wasn't the only guest unhappy with the incident. Yet she knew for sure that Karina was totally expert in her field. She'd ridden rodeo since she was a teenager and was as sure of her ground as it was possible to be. Only city slickers like Leon Powell objected to what was really the firm and fair handling of a horse.

'OK, we're coming up to a stretch where we can lope our horses.' Kirstie broke the silence with what she hoped would be a piece of good news for the guests. 'We need you to form a line. Allow some space between you and the horse ahead. And don't try to overtake.'

'Yeah, rule number one at Half-Moon Ranch!' Karina emphasised. 'No overtaking at a competitive gait!'

So Kirstie led the way up the open hillside, making flying lead changes on curves and giving her palomino his head on the straight stretches. She felt the wind tug at her light cotton shirt and long, fair hair; the exhilaration of speed and space.

When it was over, she turned Lucky round to see

13

how the guests were getting along.

Most were loping well and nicely spaced out. Only Leon Powell was messing things up.

'Might've guessed!' she muttered, watching the artist bounce around in his saddle and topple from side to side. Poor Silver Flash, wanting this rough ride to be over, was rapidly making up ground on the horse in front.

'I told you, don't overtake!' Karina yelled.

Leon snatched at the reins and yanked Silver Flash's head to one side. The big sorrel mare swerved violently off the trail, coming to a halt just short of a tall granite boulder.

'Jeez!' Powell let a string of swear words escape as he clung to his horse's neck to stay in the saddle.

Kirstie cut back across the hill, reaching him at the same time as Karina. 'You OK?'

He took a deep breath and nodded. 'That was a darned fool thing to tell me,' he accused Karina. 'What happens when I try not to overtake? Why the stupid horse just about breaks my neck!'

Karina's face was deadly serious. 'Pity.'

'Pity I didn't break my neck?' an outraged Leon Powell demanded.

There was a long silence – obviously intended to

make Powell's blood pressure rise. 'Nope. Pity Silver Flash just threw a shoe,' the wrangler said at last, gazing down at the sorrel's front left hoof.

'So?' Powell said, ready to jump down Karina's throat if she dared to say it was his fault.

'So you can't continue the ride,' she told him.

'Huh!'

'It's just one of those things. The horse will have to be walked back to the ranch.'

'You're kidding me!' Leon Powell looked round in alarm, admitting that he didn't have a clue which direction the ranch was in.

'The horse will show you,' Karina said flatly.

'Oh yeah, sure – I put my life in the hands of a dumb animal!' The artist disguised his fear with scorn. 'I'm in the middle of the Rocky Mountains and she tells me to trust my horse!'

Wow, is this guy obnoxious! Kirstie thought. 'It's OK,' she said out loud to Karina. 'I'll walk back to the ranch with Leon. You lead the rest of the group. We'll see if we can find Leon a new horse then ride out to catch you up.'

'Can't you just stick a shoe on this one?' he demanded.

'Sorry, no resident shoer at the ranch,' Karina

answered bluntly. 'OK, Kirstie, I agree.'

'But I'm missing my first ride of the week!' Powell sounded peeved. 'This is valuable research for my work. I can't afford for horses to go throwing shoes!'

Karina sighed. 'I wish I could find another way round it, Leon.' She glanced up at the cloudless blue sky, as if it would give her the patience she obviously lacked. 'But let's face it – the way things have turned out – you and Kirstie need to walk home with your horses and you're just gonna have to cowboy up!'

2

What a way to wreck a beautiful day! Kirstie thought. Walking back to the ranch with Leon Powell was turning out to be a big pain.

'Wouldn't you think they'd shoe these horses better?' he grumbled.

Then, 'How many of these are registered quarter-horses?' and, 'They don't even look like they're properly fed. You can see the ribs poking out the sides of this poor mare!'

He also talked on and on about the riding school he planned to attend in California where they would teach him to ride English, which was much more difficult than using a western saddle, and all the horses in the school would be thoroughbreds and each would be individually hot-shoed by the best blacksmith in the state . . .

Blah-blah! Kirstie tried to shut off from the alternate moaning and boasting. Looking around at the blue columbines growing in the shade of silver aspens and the white blossom of the thorn bushes, she wondered how come Leon Powell preferred to criticise rather than take in the beauty of the mountains. After all, she would've thought an artist would especially appreciate the shapes of the black markings on the slender grey trunks or the perfect bell formation of Colorado's state flower.

'As for that female wrangler!' Leon Powell was hung up on Karina. 'The way she used her spurs on that grey mare was downright brutal. To my mind, something oughta be done about it!'

Kirstie paused at the entrance to a narrow draw that would lead them out by Pond Meadow. This time she felt she needed to put Leon straight. 'Karina did the right thing back there,' she insisted. 'The situation called for some firm handling.'

'How come?' Jerking on Silver Flash's lead-rope,

Leon hustled his horse down the draw.

'Moondance is an inexperienced horse. She was already stressed out by being held up on the narrow ledge, so when she saw the mule deer she spooked big time. All Karina did was bring the horse back under control and show her there was no reason to panic. To me, that's good teaching.'

Leon sniffed and shook his head. 'I still say using spurs is a barbaric way to control your horse.'

OK, so you're a bone-headed big mouth! Kirstie thought to herself. She concentrated on finding a way out of the dead-end where Leon had led them. It meant treading carefully through an area of marsh back towards firm ground.

'Yuck!' the artist complained as his fancy new cowboy boots sank ankle-deep into the mud. Silver Flash stumbled and pulled him off-balance. Once more he yanked at the horse's head.

'Come this way.' Kirstie waited as patiently as she could, noting that Leon's outfit had taken a battering. Besides the muddy boots, the pressed blue jeans were splattered and the neat blue kerchief had unravelled. Even the light brown moustache looked a little less trim under the dusty brim of his black stetson. *Jeez, talk about city slicker!* she thought, feeling the corners of her mouth begin to twitch.

At last Leon and Silver Flash staggered through the mud to join her. 'I think I wrecked my camera!' he gasped, brushing small drops of muddy water from the leather case.

Kirstie pressed on. The sooner they reached the ranch the better.

'. . . No, it's OK, the camera's fine,' Leon reported, fussing and fumbling as he walked. He only looked up again as they emerged from the draw to see before them a glorious flower-studded meadow spread out along the side of Five Mile Creek.

'Exceptional!' he gasped, dropping Silver Flash's lead-rope. 'Where's my camera? I need to take shots!'

'Sure, no rush.' Kirstie was happy to pick up the lead-rope and wait. Maybe now that Leon had found something to please him, he would forget the moans and criticisms and become a halfway likeable human being.

And it sure was a pretty scene: the lush green grass, the snowmelt swelling the creek, the mares grazing with their foals.

'Excellent!' Leon rushed up to the fence and

snapped happily. First he zoomed in on Yukon and her new foal – a tiny brown-and-white paint like her mother, as yet without a name.

Maybe Missy. Kirstie toyed with names which might suit the foal. *Or Candy, or Matches*.

This year Yukon, Taco, Snickers and Skylark had all produced healthy foals. The first three of these broodmares were reliable old-timers on Half-Moon Ranch but for Skylark, the bay with the three-week-old foal, it was her first experience of motherhood.

'Can I go closer?' Leon asked, clambering over the fence without waiting for Kirstie's reply. His lurching action made Taco, Yukon and Snickers gather in their foals and move to a safe distance at the far side of the meadow.

Kirstie tethered Lucky and Silver Flash to the rail then climbed the fence after him. 'Would you like me to take you up close?' she asked. 'They know me, so they won't be shy.'

Leon fiddled with the buttons on his camera, then nodded. 'Try the pale brown one with the black mane.'

'The bay. Her name's Skylark. She was pregnant with the foal when we bought her last fall. It turns out the baby looks like a miniature version of the mother. Cute, huh?'

'Yeah, yeah. See if you can bring them close to the willow bushes. I could get a real good shot of the two of them backed by branches with the sun shining through.'

Kirstie nodded and approached cautiously. 'We named the baby Hummingbird because she's so small and dainty.'

'Closer!' Leon urged, his camera at the ready.

But Kirstie refused to be hurried. She began to talk gently to the mare, taking note of the body language, knowing that as long as Skylark held her head high and flicked her tail there was no chance of drawing nearer.

'Easy, girl,' she murmured soothingly, watching the angle of the mare's ears. Ears flat against the head told her that Skylark was deeply suspicious – no wonder, with Leon Powell darting about in the background. 'Ignore him,' she whispered. 'He may look strange but he's harmless.'

Gradually the sound of her voice took effect. Skylark lowered her head and eased her ears upright, though she circled round her foal to protect her.

Hummingbird also seemed to relax. Though still tiny at three weeks old she was gaining weight, growing steadier on her legs and quickly learning the meaning of a strange new world. These days she chased butterflies but steered clear of bees and she rehearsed many a hop, skip and jump with the other foals through the long grass.

'See what I have for you!' Kirstie cooed at Skylark. She'd had the foresight to take an apple out of Lucky's saddle-bag and bring it with her. If she could tempt the mother, then the foal would soon come trotting close behind.

The bay mare let her jaw go slack then slide sideways in a chewing motion. When she was still several paces away she stretched her graceful creamy-brown neck towards the apple in Kirstie's outstretched hand.

'Juicy!' Kirstie invited, standing quietly to let Skylark approach of her own free will. She could hear Leon's camera clicking busily behind her.

Skylark ducked her head. Her nostrils flared wide and her dark mane fell over her eyes as she inched forward. Then, with one look at Hummingbird to tell her to stay close, the mare moved in and snatched the prize from Kirstie's palm.

Crunch! The big teeth sank deep into the apple, while Hummingbird ventured out a couple of steps from her mom's side then quickly retreated.

'Can't you get them any closer to the willows?' Leon yelled.

The sudden, loud voice sent shock waves through the foal's skinny body. She cowered behind Skylark, who braced her legs, flattened her ears and snorted.

'I said, can't you bring them to the willows?' Thinking that Kirstie hadn't heard, Leon came bustling up to join her.

In an instant, Skylark whirled, gathered Hummingbird and loped away to join Snickers and Taco.

Kirstie said nothing, just looked at the artist, shrugged then turned away.

'I guess we'd better move on,' she told him as she reached the fence. 'You should take a look at the shots you did manage to get, then if you need some more, maybe you could come back tomorrow.'

'Did you hear the old joke about the ignorant eastern gal?' Karina asked Kirstie and her best friend, Lisa Goodman.

It was after school the next day and Lisa had come

to sleep over at Half-Moon Ranch as she often did, especially when she wanted to escape working for her mom, Bonnie, at the End of Trail Diner.

'Nope!' the girls chimed. 'I guess we never did hear the old joke about the ignorant eastern gal!'

Karina hoisted a hay bale on to the back of the pick-up truck then continued. 'Well, the gal's a city slicker from head to toe. She ain't never travelled west of Boston. So, "Mom," she says, "do cowboys eat grass?" '

Just at this point, Hadley stuck his head out of the cab to deliver the punchline in a bored, deadpan voice. ' "No, dear," says the old lady. "They're part human." '

'Gee thanks, Hadley,' Karina grumbled.

But Lisa laughed anyway. 'That's funny!'

'Yeah, except that we still get those city slickers out here, no kidding!' To prove her point, Kirstie put on a peevish male voice. ' "How do I get my horse to go?" '

Karina guffawed at the good imitation of Leon Powell. 'Well, Leon, you turn the ignition key and put your foot on the pedal!'

Amid the laughter and the slinging of more fresh bales into the truck, the artist himself strode busily by. When he spotted Kirstie he changed course and headed towards her.

'Hey, you promised me another visit to those broodmares,' he reminded her, holding up his precious camera.

Kirstie cleared her throat and brushed wisps of hay out of her fair hair. 'We're driving out to Pond Meadow right now, as it happens. Why don't you hop up into the back with us?'

'Or in the cab with me,' Hadley invited politely when he saw their guest look askance at the messy load.

So Lisa, Kirstie and Karina climbed in with the hay, all set to enjoy the slow, ten-minute drive out to the far meadow to feed the mares and foals. As the truck rolled forward along the creek trail, Karina leaned over to make conversation with Leon.

'Did you have a good day?' she hollered into the cab.

'They gave me a new horse,' Leon told her, leaning out and having to hang on to his hat in the wind. 'The blacksmith didn't show up yet to put a new shoe on Silver Flash, so I rode Crazy Horse instead.'

'Hey, nice horse!' Karina said.

'Yeah, but not a drop of breeding of any kind in his entire body!' To Leon, the bloodline obviously mattered.

'Well, that's the cowboy way,' Karina assured him. 'In the old days they never spent real money on their horses, only on their saddles.'

'They used to say, "There goes Buck with his hundred dollar saddle on his ten dollar horse!" ' Hadley added. He drummed the wheel as he spoke, finding little to say to the Californian painter.

'Tell us more about your cowgirl days,' Lisa begged Karina.

'Whadya wanna know?' Settling back against a bale of hay, the wrangler pulled her knees up to her chest and tilted her face towards the evening sun.

'Something about the horses you worked with.' Kirstie put in a request for her favourite topic.

'Well, they might not have cost much, like we said, but we sure did take good care of them – huh, Hadley?'

'What's that?' The old man poked his head out of the window as he took a bend in the track. The pick-up wobbled off-course then skidded.

'I said, we kept our horses in prime condition. A

horse would come into a ramuda at the age of four, like Moondance for example. Except all the rides on a working ranch would be geldings because most mares are bunch quitters.'

'Yeah, mares get notions of turnin' for home,' Hadley confirmed. 'That's why we gotta work with the burro on Moondance!'

'We never overworked our horses and when we trained one, we didn't expect him to be at his best until he was ten years old.'

'Wow, that's late!' Lisa said.

'So, not valuable in dollars, but you sure invested a lot of work in those guys!' Kirstie liked to hear stories from Karina's past. In her own dreams, she'd recently begun to picture growing up to become a top trainer of reining horses. She promised herself she would spend her whole life working on skills that she was only just now starting to appreciate – the sliding stops and lead changes, the pirouette turns and controlled changes of gait.

'Here we are!' Lisa cut into Kirstie's private thoughts, jumping down from the truck as it came to a halt by the gate of the meadow. Together with Karina, she slid a bale on to the ground and hauled it towards the nearest metal feeder.

Kirstie followed with a second heavy bale, looking to Leon Powell for help as he climbed down from the cab.

But the artist was too busy unzipping his camera and pressing buttons in readiness for work. He fiddled with the zoom lens while Hadley took the strain with Kirstie.

'You should get good shots today,' she called. 'These broodmares are hungry, so you can go in close without them even noticing.'

'And the light's good too.' For once, Leon Powell sounded enthusiastic.

'Does this catch me on my good side?' Lisa began to fool around by pretending to pose for the camera, fashion model style. Then, more seriously, she asked Leon how he planned to use the photographs.

'I work with them as a basis for my compositions,' he explained. 'With a digital camera I can load the images into my computer and play around with lighting and colour effects; though I still like as much atmosphere as possible from the original picture. Hold it – this is a good one of Skylark and Hummingbird.'

The bay mare loped slowly across the meadow with her foal in tow. A low sun cast long shadows across the grass but there was a golden light on Skylark's creamy-brown back, which seemed to create a sort of gentle halo round her. Her mane and tail flowed black and shiny, emphasising her delicate face and the grace of her smooth movement.

'Ahh!' Lisa laughed at Hummingbird as she tried to copy her momma. Instead of a seamless lope, the little foal could only master a hop and a skip. She was all legs, head, eyes and ears. Her dark mane and tail stuck up in fluffy tufts.

Concentrating on the splendour of Skylark, Leon

crouched down to achieve the best angle. Rapid clicks on the button captured the mare's strength and beauty. 'Excellent!' he murmured, clicking again as Skylark stopped on a slight ridge and turned to wait for Hummingbird. He caught her in profile, her neck and head in deep shadow, the sun still highlighting her back and hindquarters. 'The wind creates a beautiful movement of the mane and tail,' he pointed out excitedly. 'The whole thing looks so wild!'

'Cut the romantic stuff!' Hadley's voice rasped at Kirstie and Lisa. 'We've got mangers to fill!'

Grinning, the girls left Leon to carry on taking his artistic photographs and went to help with the chores.

'I think it's neat!' Lisa insisted as she lugged a bale towards a feeder. Yukon came nosing around for hay before it was even in the metal container. 'Get this – Half-Moon Ranch will appear in famous paintings!'

Kirstie nodded as she cut through the bale twine with a sharp knife. 'Yeah, I guess.'

'Really! Who knows, a movie star might buy one and hang it on the wall of his beach house. Wouldn't that be something?'

Kirstie lifted armfuls of alfalfa and dumped them into the manger. Snickers and Taco began to gobble greedily. Meanwhile, Skylark grew tired of posing and came to join the others. 'But they won't be paintings of the real stuff,' she pointed out.

'What real stuff?'

'Y'know – the blisters and backache, the dirt and the poop we have to scoop . . . !'

'OK, I wish I never asked!' Lisa said quickly.

They both stopped to watch Leon Powell take up another angle, capturing the four mares in a row at the manger, heads down, backs gleaming in the evening sun.

'They'll be neat paintings!' Lisa insisted. 'Whatever you think, Kirstie Scott, I reckon you should feel privileged to have a great artist like Leon Powell around!'

3

The trouble was, Leon Powell shared Lisa's high opinion of himself. He strutted about the ranch, chest puffed out, wearing his fancy boots – 'all duded-up' as Karina put it. And he expected people either to run around after him or to bow down to him and tell him he was a genius.

'Can somebody fix a light bulb in my cabin?/ bring a fresh supply of logs for the fire?/clean the mud from my five hundred dollar boots?'

Or, 'As I said to Mel/Madonna/George/Michael when they came to my Los Angeles studio to buy a painting . . .'

By Wednesday, the artist had worn his welcome pretty thin.

'Folks are beginnin' to go round him like he was a swamp.' Hadley noted that none of the guests had elected to ride intermediate with Leon that day.

Karina grinned. 'Yeah, you'd think he'd notice that he's about as welcome as a polecat at a picnic!'

'I guess being nice doesn't come into it when you're that successful.' Kirstie's older brother, Matt, joined in the chat as he helped brush down the horses in the corral. Matt was home from college in Denver and only just catching up on the week's gossip.

Kirstie had been the one to point out Leon Powell as he came down from his cabin, asked for Sandy and then went off to the ranch house to speak with her.

They worked quietly for a while, grooming, then bringing saddles out of the tack-room in a routine that went smooth as clockwork. Each horse in the ramuda had his or her own numbered saddle, plus bit and bridle. Saddles went on, cinches were tightened, without a word being said until Leon came out from the house and made it his business to interfere with the wranglers' work.

'Did someone check my cinch thoroughly?' he demanded, striding into the corral and looking in vain for his horse. 'Yesterday it was a little loose. I could've had a serious accident if I hadn't checked it myself!'

'Yessir!' Karina called. She promised to have Silver Flash tacked-up and waiting for him as soon as he'd finished breakfast.

So Leon strutted off, still cocky, in his re-pressed jeans and crisp cream shirt.

Soon after, Sandy Scott came out of the house. She was shaking her head in puzzlement as she walked across to the corral. 'Nobody told me that these artists drove hard bargains,' she mused. 'I was under the apparently mistaken impression that all they thought about was light and shade, colour, composition – fluffy stuff like that.'

Kirstie stopped raking poop into neat heaps and listened to her mom's conversation with Matt.

'You mean our friend, Leon? What kind of hard bargain did he drive?' Matt was anxious to know.

'He offered a signed, limited-edition print of the Skylark painting; in return for a week's free stay on the ranch.' Sandy shrugged. 'And guess what, I said yes!'

'Jeez, Mom!' Matt frowned. 'What does that do to our profits for the week?'

'I don't know. What's a print by Leon Powell worth? And yes – that's something I should've checked before I agreed the deal. But Leon can turn on the charm when he wants, and I guess I fell for it.'

During this conversation, Karina and Hadley had also been listening in hard. Kirstie overheard Karina mutter her verdict under her breath to Hadley. 'What a cheapskate that Leon Powell is!'

The old man went on tightening cinches. 'Who's leadin' the intermediate ride this morning?'

'Not me!' Karina broke the world speed record for answering. 'I'm with beginners. Some other poor sucker gets the pleasure of riding out with our favourite dude!'

Not me either! For once, Kirstie had been glad to go to school. Ben Marsh, their good-natured head wrangler, had done the decent thing and volunteered to take Leon out on the trail. Matt was to lead the advanced ride and had advised his group to wrap up well.

'There's a twenty per cent chance of snow,' he'd told them.

'But this is May!' someone had pointed out.

'Yeah, and we're at ten thousand feet in the Rocky Mountains!' Matt had insisted.

Typically, image conscious Leon had ignored the advice and ridden out of the corral in his usual crisp, clean shirt.

Kirstie went through the school day with nothing much to worry her. During recess Lisa hassled her over copies of the photographs which Leon Powell had taken in Pond Meadow and which she'd promised to bring in. Kirstie dug them out from the front pocket of her bag and spread them on a table for her friend to see.

'Cool!' Lisa smiled at the picture of Skylark loping lazily through the long grass. She cooed over another that included little Hummingbird bringing up the rear. There were others of the mares crowding round the manger, and close-ups of the foals with their heavy, clumsy heads and enormous, appealing dark eyes. Finally, Lisa spotted herself in one of the photographs. 'Oh no!' she cried. 'Kirstie, how come you never told me how bad I look in that pink sweatshirt!'

Kirstie studied the figure in the photo. 'You're OK,' she grunted.

'Oh yeah! I'm like a marshmallow in that thing! It's OK for you – you're so skinny you can wear whatever you want. I'm like Mom – we have, well, curves!'

Kirstie grinned. 'Come to the ranch tonight, shift bales, lick those curves into shape!'

'You bet!' Forgetting Leon's pictures, Lisa turned sideways, breathed in and studied her reflection in the window. 'You gotta help me lose seven pounds before I put on a swimsuit for the summer, OK?'

'What's new?' Kirstie asked Hadley on the ride home that afternoon.

'Karina took Moondance up Bear Hunt Trail, no problem,' the old man reported, pleased that putting his mare into the arena with the young burro seemed to be working. 'Moondance went nice and easy all the way to the end of the Overlook, as far as Monument Rock.'

'Cool. Good for Columbine. But it's partly down to the way Karina rides her, don't you think?' Kirstie knew that her praise of the wrangler was bound to raise Hadley's hackles. He and Karina had a history of bickering and fighting even though or perhaps because of the fact that they were so similar.

'She rides OK,' he conceded, quickly turning up the volume control on the radio to avoid the subject.

Lisa grinned at Kirstie and began to hum the country and western tune that was playing. They were picking up speed on the highway out of town.

'This is San Luis Sound, your Top Country Station!' the DJ declared at the end of the song.

Putting his foot on the gas pedal, Hadley began the long, slow crawl into the mountains. The road ahead snaked through a pass and beyond that, in the far distance, the white, conical cap of Eagle's Peak could be seen.

An ad for healthcare came on the radio, then one for cars' toys. 'Why pay more? Come visit CDs Plus for all your in-car sound system needs!'

Yet another song started up and this time Kirstie absent-mindedly sang along with Lisa. They were crooning the sad chorus at the tops of their voices when the DJ broke in with a weather report.

'Yeah, we know it's a freak, guys, but right here in front of me I have a severe weather warning for all you folks living south-west of Denver. That's right

– it's May and we have WEATHER on the way. One hundred per cent, sure fire and for certain!'

'Jeez!' Kirstie groaned. 'I thought they said only twenty per cent chance earlier!'

Hadley held up a finger and made her listen.

'Precipitation in the form of snow above eight thousand feet!' the DJ announced. 'Due to begin in under one hour's time. Gee, that sure caught the weather boys with their pants down! All you folks in San Luis, Renegade, Marlowe County and Colorado Springs, you wrap up well this evening, you hear!'

Grunting, Hadley switched off the radio. 'They're not the only ones caught off guard.'

Kirstie frowned. 'How come?'

'There's no one home at the ranch,' he told her. 'Your mom drove to the airport to pick up a new guest. Everyone else is out leading trail-rides.'

'And not due back until after the snow hits.' Kirstie shivered at the idea. 'Did Leon go out without a jacket again?'

Hadley nodded. 'He sure ain't gonna be happy. But I was thinkin' more about the horses than the guests.'

'Hey, quit worrying,' Lisa advised. 'A little late

40

snow never harmed those tough guys. They're built to cowboy up!'

Once more Hadley saw fit to contradict. 'You got me all wrong. I'm not talkin' about the main string. Nope – my problem is with the broodmares out in Pond Meadow. If there's no one home to drive the trailer out there and bring the mares and foals in before the snow hits, we're gonna be in big trouble.'

'Oh gee!' Kirstie's weak reaction didn't convey the lurch into anxiety she felt in the pit of her stomach. She pictured the four mares and their babies currently grazing peacefully in the green meadow, unaware of the storm that was brewing. Then the clouds drawing in over the mountains, the wind rising and the temperature falling below freezing. All in the space of sixty minutes – like Hadley said – too soon and too suddenly for comfort.

'Maybe it won't snow too hard,' Lisa suggested.

'Yeah, maybe.' Still worried, Kirstie began to scan the sky ahead. Already dark blue clouds were gathering, drawn towards Eagle's Peak which stood out unnaturally white and gleaming in what was left of the sun. 'The sky looks pretty ugly though,' she said quietly.

Hadley drove on, pushing the pick-up as fast as

41

he dared up the mountain road.

Kirstie heard the engine grind and wished they were in a vehicle that had more power and speed. 'Which way is the wind blowing?' she asked.

'From the north-west. The snow's gonna hit the ranch before it reaches us, if that's what you're wonderin'.'

'So it could be snowing there already?' Lisa muttered. Like Kirstie, she knew how thick and fast the flakes could fall. Literally within minutes the ground and the trees could be white over. In less than an hour, some of the tracks might be impassable.

And soon – too soon – before they'd even come to the turn off from the highway on to the narrow Shelf-Road, the snow had reached them.

It began as fine floating flakes that drifted lazily down from the leaden sky. They landed on the hood of the red pick-up and melted or stuck to the windscreen, to be swished off by the action of the wipers.

Kirstie peered out. As Hadley flicked the headlight switch the yellow beams picked out the swirling flakes in a kind of crazy dance, seemingly drawn towards the truck by an invisible force. The sight brought her to the edge of her seat. 'It's getting worse!'

Hadley nodded, using all his concentration to keep the truck on the rough, winding track. He'd driven this route a thousand times, could most likely do it in his sleep, but still the poor visibility and slippery, washboard surface made it difficult to go above fifteen miles per hour.

'Can you believe this!' Lisa cried. A thin layer of snow had transformed the pine trees as far as the eye could see and the bright spring flowers disappeared from the slopes. Flakes like down fell so rapidly that the whole landscape grew strangely unfamiliar.

Kirstie shook her head. She was past being able to answer out loud. *It must be six inches deep out in Pond Meadow!* she thought. And sure, the mares would cope – they'd survived worse than this. But what about the tiny foals?

At last, after some hair-raising bends, Hadley brought the pick-up to within sight of the ranch gate. A bunch of forlorn mule deer stood to the side of the road, ears pricked, watching them pass. Their straight backs were iced with snow, their antlered heads raised as if in surprise.

'What now?' Kirstie asked as the truck rattled over the cattle guard and the deer fled.

'We jump straight into the trailer and drive out to Pond Meadow,' Hadley decided. 'If we leave it much longer, there'll be no way through!'

Lisa spotted two riders descending the hill on a trail which would bring them down to the corral. Their horses half-slid, half-walked through the near-blizzard conditions. 'Who's that?'

Kirstie peered hard. 'It could be Ben on Cadillac and Leon on Silver Flash.'

Sure enough, the head wrangler and the famous guest reached the ranch at the same time as the girls and Hadley.

'Someone give me a hand!' Leon Powell demanded as he saw Kirstie and Lisa leap out of the truck. 'I'm darned near frozen to this saddle. If you don't get me down soon I'm gonna have serious frostbite!'

Yeah, like who's fault was it that you went out without a jacket? Kirstie did her best not to let her feelings show. Instead, she ran to help Leon out of the saddle. He landed with a thud, scattering loose snow all over her.

Stamping his feet, he turned to his wrangler. 'Ben,

I'm gonna need a log fire in my cabin real fast. Do you think you could fix that for me?'

Realising that there was no real question involved, Ben had to agree. After a quick word with Hadley, over the situation in Pond Meadow, he reassured himself that the old man and the girls could handle things. 'I'll get Leon fixed up, then I'll make a call to bring in Smiley Gilpin's snowplough,' he said. 'After that, I gotta make sure that Karina and Matt bring all their riders back in safely.'

Feeling relieved that help from Smiley and his Forest Rangers was on its way, Kirstie set to helping Hadley and Lisa scrape snow from the windscreen of the trailer.

The tall truck was parked down the side of the barn, facing in the wrong direction for Pond Meadow. As he climbed into the cab, Hadley yelled a fresh instruction to the girls. 'Go fetch the burro in from the arena! Put her in the rowstalls inside the barn while I turn this baby round!'

'Gotcha!' Willingly Kirstie and Lisa ran to take Columbine out of the thickening snowstorm. The small donkey gave a mournful *ee-aw*, then trotted towards them. Quickly Kirstie slipped on a headcollar and within two minutes they had her safely under shelter.

'Jeez, those poor foals!' Lisa gasped, seeing the effect that the cold had had on Columbine. The donkey shivered and trembled, hanging her head and letting the snow melt from her spiky mane into her eyes.

'Yeah, and the wind is bound to be twice as bad out in the open meadow,' Kirstie pointed out.

They raced to join Hadley, scrambling into the cab of the silver trailer and begging him to get a move on.

'Hold it!' a familiar voice cried.

Kirstie closed her eyes. *Oh no, not now, Leon!* She opened her eyes to see the guest emerging from his cabin in a bright yellow slicker, camera in hand.

'Wait for me!' he yelled. 'I decided this snow scene is too neat to miss out on!'

'What happened? I thought he had major frostbite!' Kirstie muttered.

The artist lost his footing and slid down the hill, juggling his expensive camera in one hand. 'I want to come along for the ride!' he insisted.

But Hadley already had the trailer in motion. He leaned out of the window. 'Sorry, Leon. No can do! My boss would skin me alive if I agreed to take out a guest in these conditions!'

'B-but!' Leon stood stranded in the huge tyre tracks made by the departing trailer. 'It's for my research. You can't leave me behind!'

Doggedly Hadley drove on. Snow slid in slabs from the smooth metal roof as he moved forward; the wheels churned up the pure white surface.

'Who says we can't?' Kirstie said through gritted teeth. 'We've got more important things to do than help the great Leon Powell take pretty pictures!'

4

Spring had vanished and winter returned with a vengeance. The sky was heavy with grey clouds, the gloomy air thick with giant snowflakes which whirled in the wind and settled in drifts that soon reached a depth of twelve inches.

'This wind is freezing!' Lisa gasped, leaning out of the trailer window to knock away a wedge of snow that was jamming the screen wipers. She pulled her arm in and shook more snow from her sleeve.

Hadley said nothing. He had the headlights on full-beam and leaned forward over the steering wheel in an effort to make out the route ahead.

Kirstie realised that the usual landmarks were fast disappearing. Stones to either side of the dirt track had smoothed out under a thick layer of snow, which also covered the dips and hollows in the road. She resorted to the larger boulders and trees to keep her bearings, recognising the cattle guard and wire fence which separated Red Fox Meadow from a band of National Forest land. 'How long now?' she asked Hadley as they drove under the tall arch of ponderosa pines.

Silence. Hadley's mind was on something else, his lean face set in a deep frown of concentration.

'You OK?' Kirstie murmured.

'I'm worried about Moondance,' he confessed. 'She may not be too sure-footed in the snow. I'm hoping Karina can handle it.'

'Believe me, Karina *can* handle it!' Kirstie insisted. 'She could ride that horse to the North Pole and back!'

The trailer had struggled up a slight incline and reached a sharp bend. Beyond the curve the hill dipped more steeply, back towards Five Mile Creek. Using the gear shift, instead of automatic, Hadley eased into low gear and took the dip with extreme caution.

Kirstie felt the cab tilt forward. Behind them, the empty metal horse-trailer rattled and swayed. 'What happened to the track?' she muttered.

The snow had covered the narrow road and left no sign of which route they should follow. It drove through the tree trunks at blizzard strength, whirling against the windscreen faster than the wiper blades could shift it.

'I'm gonna take a chance!' Hadley decided. 'You girls hang on!'

He eased between trees at a crawl, hoping to emerge from the forest and find a clearer indication of the track once they rejoined the creek. But the trailer brakes were under strain.

'I guess the treads of the tyres are packed with ice,' Lisa whispered, feeling the back-end of the trailer slither sideways. 'They can't get a grip on the surface.'

Hadley fought with the wheel, his foot hard down on the brake. For a few seconds he brought the giant truck back under control. But then there was a lurch at the front end as they hit a hidden obstacle. They veered off course between two trunks, with by-now useless brakes. The whole trailer jolted and slid down the rough hillside.

'Hold on!' Hadley warned again.

Kirstie and Lisa braced themselves. They were heading slowly but surely for the creek at the bottom of the hill, breaking clear of the trees then crashing through thorn bushes. The wheels churned up the fresh snow, sending sprays high into the air. Saplings snapped, the steel fender scraped rocks until finally there was an almighty splash.

'We landed in the creek!' Lisa gasped.

Nose-first, the hood pointing downwards at an angle of forty-five degrees, the back-end raised high off the ground, wheels spinning.

'You all OK?' Hadley checked.

'We're fine – not a scratch!' Kirstie assured him. She wasn't going to be the first to admit how shook-up she felt.

'What do we do now?' Lisa sighed. Nose-down in a freezing creek, in the middle of a freak blizzard, was not where she wanted to be.

Grim-faced, Hadley forced open his driver's door. It slammed against a boulder, leaving him just enough room to slide out. Landing knee-deep in ice-cold water, he waded round to the rear-end of the trailer.

'No way can we back out of here,' he reported.

'You girls are gonna have to get your feet wet!'

Relucantly Lisa opened the passenger door and plunged in, quickly followed by Kirstie. The water made them gasp and the wind almost blew them over.

Once they'd reached the bank and scrambled out, they saw just how stuck the trailer was.

'So?' Kirstie urged Hadley to make a decision. 'Do we go ahead to Pond Meadow on foot?'

The old man narrowed his eyes. 'We're not halfway there. And what good is it if we get to the meadow without the trailer? What would we do with the mares and foals – walk them all the way back to the ranch through a blizzard?'

Kirstie and Lisa shook their heads. They realised Hadley was right – they needed transport.

'We gotta run home,' Kirstie admitted. 'We can get Ben to drive the pick-up out here and tow the trailer clear of the creek.'

'Maybe.' Ducking the spinning back wheel, Hadley checked the tow-bar fixture on the fender. 'Better still if Ben already called Smiley and the Rangers are on their way with a snowplough.'

The idea gave them hope. Though the minutes were ticking by and the blizzard showing no signs of letting up, this at least was a plan to get them out of the fix they were in.

So they abandoned the trailer and hurried as fast as they could back the way they'd come. With the wind behind them and wearing hats pulled well down, they made pretty good progress through the snow.

'I hope those mares know how to shelter their foals!' Lisa said, hardly able to move her freezing lips. 'They would have to do it in the wild, before we humans came along and domesticated them, huh?'

'Yeah, but the problem there is that horses probably lived where it was hot in those days.' Kirstie thought it through. 'Sure, we've bred them specially to be able to stand colder weather. Then again, our mares have shed their winter coats, ready for summer. For them, this is like being out in a snowstorm just wearing a T-shirt and shorts!'

Lisa was silent for a while. 'But all mothers protect their young,' she pointed out. 'Won't they gather together and form a circle round the little ones to provide warmth?'

Kirstie looked to Hadley, who nodded. 'They're

smart that way,' he agreed. 'On the down side, this is one heck of a storm!'

By now they'd stumbled and skidded their way to within sight of the ranch and were able to see, dimly, plenty of activity in the corral.

'Looks like the other trail-rides are back,' Kirstie said.

'Do you see Moondance?' Hadley asked anxiously.

Kirstie tried to pick out Karina's red-and-black checkered jacket in order to reassure him. 'There!' she pointed.

Weaving in and out of the dejected horses, carrying a saddle into the tack-room, Karina seemed unaware of the crisis that had developed in Pond Meadow. 'Great weather if you happen to be a penguin!' she called when she emerged and saw Kirstie, Lisa and Hadley. Then their faces told her to quit fooling. 'What happened?' she said quickly.

'Is Moondance OK?' Hadley demanded, unable to spot his precious blue roan tethered to a rail in the corral.

'Yeah, sure.' Karina gestured for them to follow her to the barn. 'I put her in here with the burro. See for yourself.'

The old man was only satisfied after he'd taken it in with his own eyes. There, out of the cold in a stall lined with gleaming straw, was Moondance.

'I wouldn't do this for anyone else on the ramuda,' Karina teased. 'Only I know how gone you are on this particular mare.'

Allowing Hadley time to relax over Moondance, Kirstie turned as the barn door opened and Matt stepped inside.

'I just had Mom on the phone,' he told her. 'She's snowed up at Denver airport. She won't make it back tonight.'

Kirstie nodded. 'Did you speak to Ben?'

'Yeah. He just went up to the main gate to wait for Smiley to get here with the snowplough. Hey, how come you three came back without the broodmares?'

'It's a long story,' Kirstie told him. 'Let's just say we need Smiley and his plough!'

'Plus a length of strong rope,' Lisa added.

'Plus maybe shovels – and we need them fast!'

They searched in a storeroom for their tools, glad to hear the monster roar of an approaching vehicle. Running out, they were met by the sight of a giant tractor equipped with a deep, dished metal plough and driven by the broad, reassuring figure of Smiley Gilpin.

'I got here soon as I could,' Smiley said, hoisting his bulky frame out of the seat and lowering himself to the ground. He was dressed in a white stetson and dark green padded jacket with the badge and Forest Ranger logo emblazoned across the back.

Ben, Matt, Karina and Hadley immediately gathered round in a tight knot to share information and discuss priorities.

Lisa and Kirstie stood to one side.

'We gotta move!' Lisa muttered impatiently.

Kirstie gazed up into the sky, feeling flakes melt on her cheeks and eyelashes as she spoke. 'It'll soon be dusk.'

After what seemed like an age, the group of adults broke apart.

'Lisa, Kirstie – you ride in the pick-up with Hadley.' Ben issued the orders. 'You'll be following Smiley and me. Karina and Matt stay behind to take care of the rest of the horses here!'

No sooner said than they were scrambling into the two vehicles and were off. This time, when they spotted Leon Powell still dressed in his yellow slicker and hollering to be allowed to come, Hadley didn't even stop to explain. Instead, he focussed totally on following in the smooth wake of Smiley's plough.

'This is better!' Lisa gave a sigh of relief.

'Do Smiley and Ben know where we ran off the road?' Kirstie asked. Like Lisa, she felt they were making progress at last. If only the snow would ease up and the wind drop.

'They'd have to be blind to miss it,' Hadley grunted.

True, the trailer was big enough and in a stupid enough position to attract anyone's attention. As soon as they reached the top of the tree covered hill, a flash of silver told them where it was – its front end submerged, its rear-end tilted up at a crazy angle.

'Yeah!' Smiley sighed, climbing down from his cab and surveying the scene. 'Hadley, you sure drove her in real good!'

'Can you pull it out?' Kirstie asked, dragging the rope from the back of the pick-up.

'I guess,' the ranger said, slow and laid-back as ever. 'But it may take a while to figure out.'

'So can some of us go ahead on foot?' Kirstie turned to Ben with her anxious question. 'We can take lead-ropes, fetch the mares to the gate and tether them there ready for the trailer when it finally arrives.'

'Good idea,' he agreed. 'You and Lisa go on ahead. Hadley, me and Smiley will work on getting the trailer out as fast as we can. Wait at Pond Meadow for us to show up.'

Quickly fetching headcollars from Hadley's cab, they left the guys to work out the mechanics of towing the trailer out of the stream.

'At last!' Kirstie muttered, hoping that this way they could make up some of the lost time. But she knew it wasn't over yet. Once they'd battled their way through the snowdrifts to reach Pond Meadow, the hard task of catching the four mares still lay ahead.

And it was a real battle – up to their knees in snow at times, leaning into the wind, with only the winding route of Five Mile Creek to show them the way. What should have taken them five or ten minutes to walk, today took almost half an hour and there was still no sign of the rescued trailer catching them up from behind.

But in the end, in the fading light and under the bleakest of skies, Pond Meadow did come into view. Kirstie and Lisa rounded the last bend in the creek and gazed out across the flat stretch of open land.

The picture was more like Siberia than Colorado, Kirstie thought. The raw wind reached gale force as it swept down from the mountains and hit the wide valley. It whipped up the surface of the snow and made it swirl into drifts that formed craggy ridges, almost like waves on a frozen sea. And at first glance it seemed deserted.

'Where are the horses?' Lisa asked in a scared voice.

Kirstie took a deep breath. 'They've gotta be here!' she reasoned, plunging on through the snow until she reached the fence. She climbed and balanced precariously, grasping the top rail and showering fine, powdery snow to the ground. Then she vaulted over and trod into the smooth, frozen ocean that had once been Pond Meadow.

'Weird!' Lisa breathed. 'I mean, where are they?'

'Keeping under any shelter they can find if they're smart,' Kirstie answered, trying to sound calmer than she felt. 'Let's try the stand of willows by the pond.'

So they trudged to the far side, half-blinded by the snow, peering into a thicket of willow bushes all bending under their white burden. Beyond the willows, a thin covering of ice had formed at the edge of the pond, then beyond that again, the water looked black and sinister.

Still no horses. Kirstie hitched the headcollars higher on to her shoulder and went on leading Lisa towards the thicket.

The sound of their approach was dulled by the snow and wind but at last it did raise a movement from within the bushes.

Kirstie stopped and waited. The movement happened again, then a low, miserable cough. Now Lisa saw and heard it too.

'Thank goodness!' Lisa rushed ahead, making the animals retreat further into the tangle of branches and thin trunks. She hestitated and turned to Kirstie, wondering what to do.

'Let's wait here until they come out,' Kirstie suggested. 'Once they work out who we are, they'll be more confident.'

'You call them. They'll recognise your voice.'

'Easy, girls!' Kirstie said softly, waiting and watching intently. What Hadley had said seemed to be true – the mares had gathered together to shelter and protect their foals. 'You wanna come home, don't you? Out of this cold white stuff, into a nice warm barn!'

The soothing sound of her voice soon took effect. Fresh movement from the thick bushes confirmed the suspicion that more than one animal had taken shelter there. Snow fell from branches and thudded softly to the ground as dark shadows began to emerge.

It was the light sorrel coat of Snickers that Kirstie identified first. The mare stepped clear of the willows, head hanging, mane drooping, her back caked with snow. Close behind, tripping over himself in his anxiety not to be left behind, came her two-month-old dark bay foal.

'Good girl.' Kirstie held up a headcollar and let the mare approach. As soon as she drew near, she slipped on the halter. 'See, you do want to come home!'

By now, Taco too was stumbling out of the refuge, urging her foal ahead of her. Then the bushes parted again and Yukon emerged with her brown-and-white baby. Within sixty seconds, Lisa and Kirstie had gathered all three mares and their trembling offspring.

'Good job!' Lisa breathed. 'Is this it?'

'No. We still need to find Skylark and Hummingbird.' Kirstie stared into the thicket and got the strong feeling that there were no more horses in there.

'Well, here comes the trailer.' Holding tight to Taco's lead-rope, Lisa turned round to spot its approach. 'Let's take these three and come back for Skylark.'

Uneasily Kirstie agreed. Why wasn't the bay sheltering with the other mares? It didn't make sense. She took one last look into the bushes before she followed with Snickers and Yukon. Now she was certain that Skylark must have sought out a separate shelter.

'The quicker we do this the better,' she yelled after Lisa, relieved to see the three foals sticking close to their mothers as they crossed the meadow. 'I've got a bad feeling about Skylark and Hummingbird!'

'Quit worrying. The trailer made it and we already got six out of eight. This is going well!' Lisa's encouragement raised Kirstie's spirits, so that by the time they reached the meadow gate she was able to smile and greet Ben and Hadley as they stepped down from the trailer.

'It's looking good!' Ben smiled back. 'Let's get

these three girls out of this weather and into the box pronto!'

'Cut the congratulations,' Hadley told him, striding to lower the back ramp. 'You grab the other two while I take Taco. Let Kirstie and Lisa run back to bring Skylark.'

'Why – did you see where she's at?' Kirstie handed over her charges after Ben opened the gate. 'Hadley, I said, did you see Skylark?'

The old man came round the back of the trailer. He grabbed Taco's lead-rope, waited for her foal, then herded the two of them inside. 'Sure,' he told Kirstie calmly when he came out again. 'She's down a draw on the west side of the meadow. I spotted her as we drove along the creek.'

Yes! Kirstie clenched her fist. Then she tugged at Lisa's sleeve. 'Let's move it!' she cried. 'There's still one bay mare and her foal freezing to death out there!'

5

Kirstie knew exactly which draw Hadley meant. It was far away from the thicket at the edge of the pond where they'd found the other horses and it was this fact that still unnerved her as she and Lisa plunged through the snow.

Skylark's chosen place faced into the wind and though the rocky slopes rose steeply to either side, there were no trees in the bottom of the ravine to offer shelter.

'Weird!' she muttered to herself, stumbling in her haste to cross the meadow. She wondered if the other three mares had ganged up on Skylark and excluded her and Hummingbird. Maybe the new bay was low down in their pecking order and they felt that she and her foal didn't deserve to be included in their cosy group. Horses could sometimes be mean that way.

'Poor things, they must be so cold!' Lisa clutched her collar close round her throat and put her head down to protect her face from the wind. 'Oh Jeez, I forgot to bring a headcollar,' she said suddenly.

'I have two.' Kirstie held them up. By this time they were approaching the entrance to the draw and she had to work out the best way to come round a group of large boulders and appear before the waiting horses without startling them. 'Wait,' she told Lisa, who was all for running ahead.

'OK, gotcha.' Lisa stopped. 'Go ahead, call Skylark's name.'

Kirstie spoke gently, easing past the boulders, reassuring Skylark that the ordeal would soon be over. 'We're sure sorry that it took so long,' she told her. 'This storm is such a freak that it caught everyone off-guard – Mom, Matt, even Hadley.'

From down the draw, still out of sight, she heard a horse take a deep breath then let out a long, shuddering sigh. Kirstie glanced over her shoulder, nodded at Lisa and continued.

She scrambled to the top of the final boulder and looked down into the draw. Snow blew down the narrow channel, half-blinding the girls, so it was a while before they made out the shape of the mare keeping a shivering guard over her foal. When they finally picked her out, they saw that she was sideways on, turning her head slowly towards them and standing over Hummingbird, who lay motionless in the snow.

Kirstie felt her stomach twist. She launched herself from the boulder and ran towards the two horses, catching one of the halters on a sharp spur of rock and wrenching her arm. A muscle in her shoulder burned with a sharp pain.

Lisa was slower to make sense of the scene. Then she realised there could be only one reason why Hummingbird had collapsed and why Skylark was making no attempt to urge her to her feet. 'Oh no!' she groaned, overtaking Kirstie and dropping on to her knees beside the lifeless form.

The mare stood still as stone. *Too late*, she seemed to say.

Kirstie too went on to her knees. Desperately she began to scrape soft snow from Hummingbird's

face, uncovering her mouth and softly brushing flakes from her closed eyelids.

Lisa took off her jacket, swept snow from the foal's thin body and carefully covered her. 'Wake up,' she pleaded, massaging her neck with a circular motion.

Too late! The droop of Skylark's head told them clearly that nothing they did now would make her foal open her eyes again. She lowered her face to touch Kirstie's hand. *Hummingbird is dead.*

'She froze to death,' Kirstie told her mother.

Sandy Scott had waited for the ploughs to clear the roads out of Denver, then battled through to the ranch with their new guest – a lawyer friend of Leon Powell called Ron Waterson. They'd finally made it home in the grey dawn light of Thursday.

'I know, honey. I'm sorry.' They sat round the kitchen table, coming to terms with the events of the day before.

'Poor little thing!' Lisa sighed. She and Kirstie had spent a restless night, unable to get to sleep for thinking about and crying over Skylark's foal.

They knew they'd done everything possible out there in the meadow – tried to bring warmth back into the frozen body, massaged her chest to restart the still heart. Lisa had even run to fetch Ben and Hadley from the trailer. The guys had hurried across to find Kirstie still forlornly working on the foal.

Ben had taken one look and told her it was no good. Hadley had stooped to draw Lisa's jacket over Hummingbird's face. Then he'd helped Kirstie to her feet. 'The foal's been dead for quite a while,' he'd said gently. 'Look at the mother – she knows it for sure.'

And they'd had to accept it. Ben had picked up the stiff, light body and carried it to the trailer, while Hadley led Skylark. The mare had let the men do as they wished, as if all the spirit had gone out of her. She'd walked mournfully across the meadow, dark mane drooping over her face, snow settling on her swaying back.

'I understand you're hurting about this,' Sandy told the girls now. 'But look at the good things you achieved yesterday. You saved seven out of eight horses who would otherwise have died. That's gotta be something to be proud of!'

'Yeah, but if only we hadn't left Skylark and Hummingbird till last!' Kirstie couldn't forgive herself. She kept rerunning events and trying to come out with a different result.

'If only I hadn't been snowed up in Denver. If only Ben had decided to cancel the afternoon trail-rides because of the increasing chance of snow . . .' Sandy sighed. 'What's the point of "if only" is what I'm saying.'

Kirstie stared at her breakfast untouched on the plate.

'Eat!' Sandy urged gently.

But the food seemed to float and grow fuzzy as Kirstie's eyes filled with tears. 'Sorry.' She shook her head, stood up and walked quickly out of the house.

That was the problem with crying – the more you told yourself to quit, the hotter your face grew and the quicker the tears came anyway. When it happened to Kirstie, she preferred to be alone.

So she ventured out into the snowy morning, dressed only in sweatshirt, jeans and boots. She would go to the barn and check the horses, but skirt round the corral so she didn't have to talk to anyone who might be there.

'What's gonna happen with the weather today?' she heard Leon Powell asking Karina, who stood on the tack-room porch. The artist had his friend, Ron Waterson, with him and today both men wore padded ski jackets and warm woollen hats.

'Snow's gonna melt by midday!' Karina told them. 'So you can pack away your ski suits and dig out the old spurs and chaps. We'll all be out riding soon as it clears up.'

'How about this morning?' Leon persisted, obviously unhappy that he would have to wait a whole four hours to show Ron the trails.

Kirstie walked quietly on. She thought of how Hummingbird's life had hardly started. The little foal had only seen the spring flowers unfold and the grass grow green for a few short weeks. She'd become part of that wonderful rhythm of nature, only to have her world turn white and hostile and be suddenly robbed of all the things she would have experienced as she grew up.

That was the saddest thing – the briefness of her life. And of course, the way Skylark pined now that she was gone.

Quietly Kirstie opened the barn door and walked down the central aisle. The atmosphere was peaceful – the burro and Moondance in their neighbouring stalls and the three broodmares across the aisle, fussing over their foals. She had to walk to the end, to the towering stack of alfalfa bales and the final stall in the row, to find Skylark.

This stall too was quiet. But it wasn't a good silence. Kirstie found the bay mare standing stock-still, her face turned into a dark corner, her whole body drooping. There was no reaction as Kirstie opened the door.

'I know,' she murmured, noting the strange absence of interest – the face to the wall, head down, eyes and ears taking in nothing around her. It was the way horses behaved when they were real sick. 'It's the worst thing.'

Skylark closed her eyes and dropped her head lower still. Everything about her was stiff, dull and faded, as if overnight she'd become ancient.

'But it's not your fault,' Kirstie whispered, laying a hand on her neck. 'You stayed out there with her until the end and I'm sure Hummingbird was less scared because of that. Now it's just tough being without her.'

The lonely, grieving mare opened her eyes and turned her head. Her gaze was empty, dark and sad. It almost broke Kirstie's heart in two.

* * *

'No school today.' Lisa met Kirstie on the house porch, coming out to meet her as she returned from the barn. 'I guess that's good news, huh?'

Kirstie kicked off her boots. 'How come? Didn't the ploughs get through to San Luis?'

'Yeah but Mom just called to say school's cancelled. The water main froze and burst, so there's no water supply to the whole site until they fix it.' There was no sign of Lisa's normal bubbly energy as she reported the situation. Her round, freckled face was serious and there was a worried look in her grey eyes.

'I heard Karina telling Leon that the snow will be gone by midday,' Kirstie told her in return. Somehow this made the fierce cold snap that had killed Hummingbird all the more cruel. Within twenty-four hours, once the snowmelt had been carried away in the creeks and rivers, it would be spring again and the meadow would look for all the world like nothing had happened.

'Talking of which . . .' Lisa raised her eyebrows for Kirstie to turn round and see who was coming towards the ranch house.

It was the artist and his lawyer friend, talking earnestly between themselves, followed at a wary distance by Karina. 'Give me strength!' Kirstie muttered, predicting to herself that Leon was about to launch into yet another complaint.

'Hey Kirstie, I need to see your mom!' he called.

'Let me get her for you,' she volunteered quickly. 'Just wait a moment, please.' Better to keep him outside in the cold than let him into the house where he might take off his jacket, sit down and chew off Sandy's ear in comfort.

She slipped inside. 'Mom, Leon Powell is here. Looks like he's got another problem. I think it's about not being able to ride this morning.'

Sandy came out of her small study that led off from the hall. She smiled faintly and went out.

'Sandy, how're you doing? Listen, we just heard what happened yesterday!' The artist came up on to the porch and stood close to Kirstie's mom.

'What d'you mean?' Something about his bustling, hustling manner put Sandy on her guard.

'You know – the foal in the meadow,' Leon muttered. 'I guess you didn't want the news to leak out but motor-mouth Karina just let it slip.'

Sandy frowned. 'We weren't trying to keep it quiet, Leon. Why should we?'

Karina, who had been hanging back, now stepped

forward. 'That's what I tried to tell him,' she cut in. 'Like, why should it be a secret? It was one of those things. Tough. But hey, it happens.'

Her interference seemed to get Leon steamed up. 'Typical!' he protested. 'That's what I've come to expect from her. She has about as much feeling for these horses as I do for my bank manager, which is zilch!'

'I'm sure Karina didn't mean it like that—' Sandy began.

'Sure she meant it. I've seen her kick her horse until its sides bled!'

'No way!' It was Kirstie's turn to break in. 'I mean, Mom, that isn't true!'

Sandy folded her arms and hunched her shoulders. 'So what would you like to say about the foal that died, Leon?' she asked as evenly as she could.

'I'd like to get to the bottom of it,' he said.

'*I, I, I*'! Kirstie was sick of hearing him say the word. She knitted her brows and waited for him to stop talking and go away.

'First off, I understand that the foal froze to death out there.'

Slowly Sandy nodded.

'Which suggests to me that the business of bringing in these horses was badly handled. Look, it's no big deal to get out there in a trailer and pick them up, yet you people delayed until it was too late for one of the babies. I mean, how does that look? Not good, huh?'

Kirstie felt every word stab at her. 'Badly handled', 'no big deal', 'too late'. The judgements struck home and for a while she was convinced that for once Leon was right.

'So what are you suggesting?' Sandy still held on to her temper but it was growing visibly strained.

'I'm telling you that you should take another look at your staff because somehow, somewhere amongst the wranglers, poor judgement yesterday led to a defenceless animal's unnecessary death!'

This was what Leon Powell had been working up to saying and now that it was out in the open he stood back to enjoy its effect.

Sandy took a step back, then recovered. 'You're accusing my guys of neglect!' she said in disbelief.

Leon sniffed. 'What else? Ron and I have discussed it and it's the only conclusion we can reach.'

Kirstie glanced at Leon's lawyer friend – a grey-haired man with a grey face and expressionless eyes. He was thin, tall, quiet and totally unreadable.

'Now hold on just a minute!' Karina advanced on to the porch, one hand held up like a traffic cop. 'When you say "neglect", who exactly are you pointing the finger at here?'

Leon stared her out. 'I'm not naming names – yet. I just want to know exactly what happened.'

'It snowed. A foal died, for Chrissakes!'

Kirstie felt her mouth go dry as things turned really nasty.

'Karina, please—!' Sandy stepped between her and Leon.

'Oh listen, this is total garbage!' the wrangler went on. 'We got a guy here who to my mind ain't never been on a horse in his life before. He struts around the place givin' orders, mouthin' off about somethin' he knows nothin' about! And now we have to stand here and listen to this stuff about neglect!'

'Karina, you're not helping here!' Sandy pleaded again for her to be quiet. 'Leon, if you and Ron would like to come into the house, I'm sure we can work through this calmly and logically.'

'Oh, like yeah!' By this time, Karina had lost it. 'Leon doesn't know the meaning of logic!'

She was about to turn on her heel and storm off when Leon quickly sidestepped into her path. 'Lady, I got your number!'

'Well, good for you!' she countered, vaulting over the rail on to the ground.

'You saw that – that was threatening behaviour!' Leon appealed to Ron. Then he turned to Sandy. 'To be honest, I don't see the point of any more talk on the subject. In fact, I've had it with this place. C'mon, Ron, let's go!'

'Please, Leon!' Sandy followed him down the step. 'Let's not overreact.'

'Yeah and let's not sweep things under the carpet,' he argued back. 'You gotta understand – I'm an animal person. I care for wildlife and the correct care of domesticated creatures. It's one of my major principles in life!'

'I understand, I really do.' Desperate to calm things down, Sandy's face showed the strain.

'The truth is, Sandy, I don't care to stay here any longer. I'm going back to my cabin, I'm gonna pack my bags and leave!'

'But we have a deal!' she protested. 'A piece of

your artwork in return for your free stay on the ranch!'

'Forget it,' he snapped, striding away with Ron Waterson in tow. 'I'm outta here. What's more, I've made up my mind to make an official complaint to the Dude Ranch Association. Soon your reputation will be smashed!'

Kirstie saw her mom sag and sigh, stranded in the trampled snow as Leon Powell stormed off.

'Oh!' He stopped, turned and made his final, puffed up, off-the-wall announcement. 'And by the way, you can expect a direct legal challenge from my friend Ron here.'

'What kind of legal challenge?' Sandy asked.

Powell delivered it straight. 'I'm charging you, Sandy Scott, with deliberate neglect. Next time I see you will be in court!'

6

The snow that had killed Hummingbird melted into Five Mile Creek and swelled its banks to bursting point. Soon all that was left were rapidly shrinking white patches against bright green grass and trees. The last wet avalanches slid and fell from the edges of the red barn roofs.

By midday on Thursday, Ben Marsh was rounding up wranglers and helpers into the corral to saddle horses for the afternoon ride.

The request for help pulled Kirstie and Lisa out of the gloomy mood that had settled on them since Leon Powell's stormy exit. It felt better to have work to do and something practical to concentrate on, even if Kirstie could still hear the wildlife artist's threat ringing in her ears. So she dragged heavy saddles from the tack-room, slid them on to the horses' broad backs and calmly and efficiently tightened cinches.

'Hey Ben, forget about Silver Flash,' Lisa called to the head wrangler as he tacked-up the big sorrel. 'Leon Powell walked out on us!'

'He did?' Nothing seemed to surprise Ben, or to excite his curiosity. He simply shrugged and carried the saddle back to the tack-room. 'What about his buddy – the guy who just got here?'

Lisa shrugged. 'I don't know what happened to Ron Waterson.'

'I stuck around,' a voice said from the corral fence. Waterson was coolly informative, giving nothing away. The opposite to Leon Powell in both looks and personality, he merely observed the routine of the wranglers and melted into the background.

Lisa gave Kirstie an eye-swivelling look. 'Whadya bet he's a plant?' she hissed.

Kirstie looked puzzled.

'Y'know, a plant! Our friend Leon left Ron behind

so he could spy on us for the court case and report back.'

'Maybe.' Right now, Kirstie couldn't care less. All she wanted was for the afternoon groups to ride out so that she could go and spend some time with Skylark.

'Have you ridden before, Ron?' Ben asked in his friendly manner.

'Some.'

'English or western?'

'Western. I visited a ranch near Renegade last fall, and one in Montana last spring.'

'Well, Ron, d'you reckon you could handle Silver Flash yourself since Leon left early?'

Waterson nodded and the arrangements were made for him to join Ben's own group. Soon the other guests strolled down to the corral from their cabins, found their horses ready and waiting, mounted, then eagerly formed their groups to depart.

'Are you and Lisa coming?' Karina asked Kirstie, as she fetched Moondance out of the barn. Hadley's blue roan looked sleek and eager, despite the old man's worries of the previous day.

Both Kirstie and Lisa shook their heads.

Karina looked at them shrewdly. She hopped into the saddle then rode Moondance across the corral to where they stood. 'Listen, don't let the Leon Powell garbage get to you,' she said in a loud voice. 'A guy like that ain't got a lick of cow sense. Quit frettin', there ain't the ghost of a chance he'll do what he said about bringin' in the law!'

Obviously, the straight-talking wrangler hadn't spotted Ron Waterson amongst Ben's group of riders. Kirstie winced and told her to hush. Waterson himself had heard but showed no reaction.

Karina hadn't finished her say. 'I'm telling you – Powell took his pictures, did his research and got a free vacation out of us. Call me a cynic, but I reckon that's what he planned all along.'

'Er-hum!' Lisa coughed and did her eye-swivel towards the lawyer.

Thankfully, it was time for the rides to leave.

'OK, so I have a big mouth!' Karina added, catching on at last. 'But I still say I'm right, huh, Matt?' Looking round for an ally, she caught sight of Kirstie's brother crossing the yard towards his car. 'What's the betting Leon Powell doesn't get as far as the courtroom door over this Hummingbird thing!'

'I'd lay five dollars on the line that he does,' Matt contradicted. 'With a guy like that, the more noise he can make the better he likes it. If he believes he can stir things for us and at the same time get some high profile media coverage for himself and his work, that's exactly what he'll do.'

As the argument swung this way and that, Kirstie and Lisa slipped away into the barn where Columbine screeched her objection to having been left behind by Moondance. Then the little donkey shoved her nose between the gaps in the timber wall of her stall, demanding to be stroked as the girls went by.

'Hey, honey!' Lisa leaned over and patted the burro's furry back. 'Moondance will soon be home. Maybe I should take you out to the arena for some exercise?' She turned to Kirstie, who nodded.

'You do that. I'll say hi to Skylark.' Walking on, Kirstie hoped to find more signs of life from the grieving mother. An improvement in the mare would at least be one glimmer of light in a dark day. But no – Skylark still kept to her far corner, refusing to face the door. Her haynet was untouched, her manger full of unwanted grain.

'C'mon, you gotta eat,' Kirstie pleaded, sidling

into the stall. 'Y'know, there's nothing we can do about yesterday. It's over.'

Skylark inched her head round, giving Kirstie that same dull, empty look.

'OK, so I don't know how it feels. Is that what you're saying? Well, I guess that's right. But how bad do you imagine I feel about leaving you and Hummingbird out there so long? I mean, I'd have given anything to get there sooner – we all would. Only, you weren't there with the others. We had to come back and find you, and those extra few minutes probably made all the difference . . .'

Skylark gave a shuddering sigh and Kirstie stopped.

There was silence. Chinks of sunlight filtered through the outside wall of the barn and a pair of blue jays hopped noisily over the high tin roof.

Something didn't sound quite right to Kirstie about the few extra minutes remark. What was it? A comment Hadley had passed in order to comfort them. 'The foal's been dead for quite a while. Look at the mother – she knows it for sure.'

Right! Kirstie thought. There'd been no frantic appeal from Skylark as she and Lisa had rounded the entrance to the draw. And a sheet of snow already covered the foal from head to foot. It had only been shock and disbelief that had made them brush off the snowflakes and attempt to revive her. In her heart she'd known all along that it was futile.

Dead quite a while. Say, for half an hour before they even reached Pond Meadow. Which would explain why Skylark hadn't joined the other mares and foals in the shelter of the willow thicket. Hummingbird would have been too weak to make it to the far side of the meadow – a distance of maybe three hundred yards.

Quite a while. Maybe longer than thirty minutes. Perhaps even before the blizzard had set in?

Kirstie pictured the frail little foal collapsing in the draw for some other reason. Skylark had done her best to raise her to her feet again but she'd failed. When the snow and the wind had come, she'd stayed with her foal while the other horses crossed to the pond. She'd kept a guard, stood in silent vigil over her already dead or dying foal!

'So why didn't Skylark take Hummingbird to the thicket?' Kirstie demanded. Her grey eyes sparked and challenged Lisa to answer.

'Because – because she didn't!' Lisa backed away

from Kirstie's intense gaze, carrying on pitching flakes of hay into the burro's outdoor manger.

'That's no answer at all!' To Kirstie it now seemed so obvious. And so vitally important. 'Think about it, Lisa. A mare has to have a big, big reason for not taking shelter when she gets the chance. And the only thing that would do it would be if her foal was in some kind of danger. You see what I'm saying?'

Lisa finished with the hay then sighed. 'No, I don't. And y'know, what, I don't see why you're so hung up on it.' She frowned, then said with a quiver in her voice, 'Face it, Kirstie – the foal's dead. Period.'

Tossing her fair hair back over her shoulders, Kirstie bulldozed ahead. 'That's not the issue. The point is, exactly when did Hummingbird die?'

Blocking her ears and walking away, Lisa seemed to be almost in tears. 'What difference does it make?' she yelled over her shoulder. 'Why obsess over the details? Honest, Kirstie, just let it go.'

Kirstie caught up with her in the empty yard in front of the house. 'What difference does it make?' she echoed. 'It makes all the difference in the world, if it happened another way. Say, for instance, it wasn't the cold that killed Hummingbird . . . !'

'Oh c'mon! It was below zero out there, plus the wind chill. There was a blizzard. Of course Hummingbird froze to death!'

Now it was Kirstie's turn to sigh and frown. 'OK, so now I know where I stand with you, Lisa. If you don't want to help solve this mystery, that's fine with me!'

Lisa's voice rose to a high pitch. 'Mystery? What mystery? This thing is plain as my nose. And it hurts to drag it up. All I want to do is forget!'

'OK, OK, walk away, why don't you?' Kirstie too was close to tears. She couldn't believe that she was arguing with her closest friend. And yet Lisa was actually turning her back, walking up into the house, shaking her head.

'I'm gonna call Mom to come and fetch me,' she muttered quietly in a flat voice that put an end to the row once and for all. 'Call me when you're over this, OK.'

She left Kirstie standing stunned in the yard, looking up at white clouds scudding across a blue spring sky, feeling that one of the people she most relied on in the entire world had walked out on her and she didn't understand why.

* * *

Once Lisa had gone, Kirstie was alone on the ranch. She'd watched Bonnie Goodman drive out through the main entrance, aware that a rift the size of the Grand Canyon had opened up between her and Lisa. *Well, let it,* she'd tried to tell herself but deep down she'd felt scared and confused.

So straightaway she'd looked around for the next person she could convince. It couldn't be Karina, Ben or her mom, who were out leading rides. Perhaps Hadley, who might be around doing chores in the barn or tack-room. She'd searched them and found no one. Anyhow, his pick-up wasn't parked in its usual spot, if she'd bothered to look. Like Matt, he'd most likely driven off on an errand.

She was all by herself and the new idea about Hummingbird was burning inside her head. Of course it mattered when and how the foal had died. Only, Lisa had been too emotional to take it in. It linked up directly with the nasty accusation from Leon Powell and the threatened legal action. Sure it did – anyone except Lisa would see that. Especially someone who could come up with other ways in which the foal might have died . . .

A fresh thought drove Kirstie to run out and bring Lucky in from Red Fox Meadow. She tacked him up and pointed him north towards the Shelf-Road, dredging up a vague memory of Matt saying over lunch that he planned to borrow Smiley Gilpin's road grading machine and get out on to the dirt road to level the surface. It was a job that could only be done after rain or melted snow, when the ground was soft as clay under the wide metal grader.

Kirstie knew that if she bushwhacked up the hill, east of the ranch entrance, she would reach the Shelf-Road faster. So she let her palomino know that this was urgent, setting him off at a brisk trot and easing him into a lope as soon as the pine trees that sheltered the ranch thinned out. Lucky obliged, taking her at a smooth gallop along the first stretch of dirt road until it reached a fork, which would lead in one direction on to the highway and in the other towards the Ranger's cabin on Timberline Trail.

Here Kirstie stopped. She could see from the clear tyre tracks and ridges in the road that Matt had not yet driven the grader down to the junction. By turning towards Red Eagle Lodge, she should meet him on the route. If she listened hard, she might even hear the giant machine on its way down the trail.

Or if she didn't pick up the unusual sound, her horse might. Sure enough, when she faced Lucky up the hill, he raised his head high and pricked his ears. There was something different up there from mule deer and coyotes – a sound like thunder, but with a mechanical roar. Lucky flicked one ear towards Kirstie, as if waiting to be told what to do next.

She clicked her tongue and set him off once more, loping for another half mile round tight bends, beneath low branches from overhanging trees, until she eventually found what she'd been looking for.

The grader appeared as a yellow metal monster emerging from dense trees, its single front claw raised and glinting in the sunlight. Trundling on caterpillar tracks, it lumbered down the slope, roaring monotonously.

Kirstie felt Lucky tense up at the sight. He snorted loudly then flattened his ears and tail tight to his body, ready to run.

'Easy, boy. It won't hurt you.' Normally Kirstie would have avoided stressing her horse and held him back from the machine. But today she really needed to talk to Matt. So she ordered Lucky forward on a tight rein, trying to convey her own confidence and command of the situation. Reluctantly this time, he obeyed.

They approached cautiously, waiting for Matt to hit a curve on the track where he could spot them. When his figure appeared inside the high cab, Kirstie raised her hand and hailed him.

Matt saw horse and rider straight away. He stopped the grader and cut the engine. Then he waited for Kirstie and Lucky to lope towards him.

'Hey!' She was breathless and the words came spilling out. 'Matt, what if the cold didn't kill Hummingbird? What if it was something else? What would that something be?'

'Hold it,' he implored, climbing down from the mud spattered grader. 'Sure it was the cold. It had to be.'

Don't give me that! Kirstie thought. *I've already been through that with Lisa!*

But Matt had already taken one step her way. 'Hey, if the foal didn't freeze to death that makes Leon Powell's thing about neglect look shaky, huh?'

Kirstie nodded. She could have flung both arms round practical, logical Matt's neck. Instead, she jumped down from the saddle and walked right up to him. 'So what else could it have been?' she asked more quietly.

'An accident,' he suggested. 'A falling rock, a fatal injury.'

'An attack by a mountain lion?' She knew that this scary predator could easily bring down a weak foal. Even a small pack of coyotes could do it if they took the mother off-guard. 'But I didn't see any visible injuries.'

Matt nodded. 'Well it could be a virus, or an inherited genetic condition that the foal was born with – any one of a hundred things.'

Kirstie let out a long, deep sigh. Now that she had Matt agreeing with her, she hit a problem that she hadn't foreseen. 'How are we going to find out for sure?' she asked.

Her student-vet brother was ready with an instant and hyper-clinical reply

'That's easy,' he said. 'Glen Woodford sent a car up to the ranch first thing this morning. The driver collected the body and took it to town for incineration. All I need to do is give him a call and ask him to perform an autopsy before he disposes of the corpse.'

7

'What's wrong, honey?' Sandy asked at breakfast next morning. 'You're not still breaking your heart over Skylark's foal?'

Kirstie shook her head. She and Matt had agreed not to say a word to their mom about their new theory, so as not to raise her hopes. Matt had pointed out that if the autopsy confirmed death by hypothermia, then they were still in deep trouble with Leon Powell. And then what would have been the point of telling Sandy?

But Kirstie was having a bad time with the autopsy idea. She'd reckoned she wasn't the squeamish type – that she could handle injuries, blood and emergencies as well as the next person. She'd even thought about following Matt to vet school when the time came. Now she realised it wasn't that easy. Sometimes animals died and had to be gruesomely examined in a lab. The idea made her feel sick and unhappy. No, she would never be able to handle that part, she decided.

'So eat!' Sandy recommended, pushing a plate of pancakes towards her.

Kirstie looked up and managed a faint smile. 'You sound like me when I'm talking to Skylark!'

'Exactly. So go ahead, don't give yourself a hard time over this.' Sandy took a paper-knife to the morning's delivery of mail, opening envelopes and snatching gulps of coffee in between times. 'What happened to Lisa by the way?'

'She had to go home.' Kirstie's reply was vague. 'Her mom needed her in the diner, I guess.'

'Don't give me that. You broke friends,' Sandy said shrewdly. 'I just have to look at your face to know it.'

'What's wrong with my face?' Kirstie felt herself go hot all over. She pretended to attack the pancakes in order to avoid her mom's gaze.

'It's shut up like a clam,' Sandy pointed out, slicing open the last envelope in the pile. 'And you're moping around feeling lonesome and blue, even though you just had the official verdict of no school again today.'

As she spoke, her voice began to tail off. She narrowed her eyes and read the letter.

'What is it?' Kirstie asked, breaking free of her own preoccupations.

'Nothing.' Sandy stood up and swept the mail into a pile. 'No problem. I have to make a phone call.'

But Kirstie jumped up from the table and stopped her mom from leaving the room. 'If I admit that I broke friends with Lisa, will you tell me what's in that letter?' she challenged.

Still Sandy shook her head.

'OK, let me guess. It's from Leon Powell's attorney.'

Her mom sighed. 'Not quite. This is from the Dude Ranch Association, informing me that they've received a serious complaint about the treatment of our horses. They understand that the matter is being taken to court. Meanwhile, they'd like to send someone to take a look at our horse management and staff training programme.'

Kirstie frowned. 'Leon Powell really meant what he said,' she muttered.

Sandy braced herself. 'Yeah, but let's not get hung up on this,' she told Kirstie firmly. 'You feed the barn horses while I make my phone call. We still have a ranch to run, remember!'

'Nothing!' Matt shook his head and shot out the word before Kirstie had even opened her mouth.

She'd spotted her brother in the tack-room as she'd been heading for the barn. She'd changed course suddenly, woven between the horses tethered at the rails and come face to face with him on the porch.

'No news from Glen Woodford?' she double-checked. 'Are you sure?'

'Yeah.' Matt rested a saddle on a nearby rail. 'I called him last night and left a message on his answer machine. He hasn't got back to me yet.'

'Shouldn't you call him again?' Kirstie quizzed. 'You need to speak to him direct.'

Matt shook his head. 'Vets are busy people. He must've been out on another visit but he would pick up the message when he got back. It's all in hand, no problem!'

'But . . . !' Kirstie wanted answers from the autopsy and she wanted them now.

'We wait!' Matt insisted, lifting the saddle and stepping down into the corral. 'Don't you have work to do?' he called back.

She remembered the horses in the barn and scooted to fetch them their hay and grain.

'You thought I wasn't coming, huh?' she said to Taco, Yukon and Snickers, who stood waiting at their mangers, their hungry faces turned in her direction. Quickly she delivered their alfalfa and watched them start to munch. Behind them, their foals hopped and skipped, testing out their muscles and just plain enjoying life.

Kirstie smiled sadly, thinking of poor Skylark. She moved on quickly with another load of hay, determined to tempt the lonely bay mare to eat. But she found her lying on her side, her head resting against the hay, with a listless air hanging over her.

'Come on, Skylark, get up, there's a girl!' Kirstie urged, fluffing the pale hay in the manger causing the sweet smell to drift across the stall.

The mare twitched her black tail and flicked her ears, making no attempt to stand.

'C'mon, this is making you sick,' Kirstie declared.

'We can't let it happen. You've gotta make an effort.'

Skylark responded by raising her sorrowful head.

'Good girl, easy does it!'

The horse twisted sideways and threw her weight forward. Soon she was on her knees and then up on her feet.

'Cool!' Kirstie murmured. 'Now I can brush you and get the hay out of your mane, make you look pretty.'

She did as she promised, taking the dust out of Skylark's beige coat and picking straw out of her dark hair. After half an hour the horse was presentable once more.

But still she wouldn't eat. Even when Kirstie offered her hay in the palm of her hand, she turned her head away and sighed.

'OK, so now we go for a walk.' Deciding not to force it, instead Kirstie grabbed a headcollar and led Skylark out of the barn. Pining for her foal or not, she still needed fresh air and exercise. Kirstie put on speed as they passed the three other broodmares and their babies to spare Skylark the sight of the happy, healthy foals.

'Remember Columbine?' She spoke to the mare in a bright, chatty way as she led her across the by-now empty corral. 'Hadley reckons the burro is good for Moondance. What d'you think?'

They stopped by the arena, looking in through the rails at the young donkey. Columbine was alone, deserted by Hadley's blue roan for another morning on the trail with Karina. When she saw Kirstie and Skylark, she trotted eagerly towards them.

'Cute, huh?' Kirstie said with a smile. 'Look at her tiny feet and big pointy ears. Say, how about you keeping her company for a while?'

Kirstie opened the gate and led Skylark into the arena, releasing her from the headcollar and turning her loose.

Straight away the burro made friendly advances. She reached up and sniffed the mare's neck and face, then when that didn't work, she put in a small hop and buck to claim attention. Still no response from Skylark. So Columbine took another sniff then tried a definite nudge with her nose.

The mare turned her head away.

'Be nice!' Kirstie whispered. 'Can't you see, Columbine likes you?'

Nothing she said made any difference. Skylark was determined to ignore Columbine.

'Tough,' a guy's voice said from beyond the fence.

Kirstie frowned then went to find out who had been watching. She discovered Ron Waterson, dressed in city clothes, holding an attaché case under his arm. At first she bristled, then told herself not to show her dislike. 'How come you didn't go trail-riding?' she asked.

The Man in Grey shrugged. 'I have a meeting in town. A car is coming to collect me.'

What kind of meeting? Where? Does it have to do with Leon Powell? Questions flooded Kirstie's mind, but she managed not to open her mouth. After all, Ron Waterson wasn't likely to give any answers. He stood there, blank faced, glancing at his wristwatch and studying Skylark.

'Is that the mare who lost the foal?' he inquired, as if to make sure of his facts.

Kirstie nodded. 'I'm worried about her. She's missing Hummingbird. This was her first foal, so she's real cut up.'

'Hmm.' The lawyer grunted then spotted his chauffeur driven car on the drive. He walked slowly to meet it.

'Will you be back?' Kirstie called, wondering about dinner tonight and Ben's list of horses for tomorrow.

Ron paused. 'Oh sure,' he confirmed, his back

towards her, his voice giving nothing away as usual. 'You can bet your bottom dollar I'll be here!'

The rest of the morning passed quietly. Kirstie left Skylark out in the sunshine, occasionally looking in on her in the arena to find the burro chasing his own shadow in cute, zigzagging bursts of speed and the mare standing quiet and subdued as ever. Seeing this, Kirstie would shake her head sadly and move on to her next chore.

Once or twice Hadley too passed by, took a look and grunted.

Come midday, just before the rides were due back, the old wrangler poked his head out of Ben's office in the tack-room and hailed Kirstie. 'Is Matt around?' he yelled.

She was raking the yard but stopped and went across. 'No. Why? Was that the phone?'

Hadley nodded. 'The veterinary wants to speak with Matt.'

'Glen Woodford? It's OK, let me talk to him!' She squeezed past and rushed to pick up the phone. This was it – the news on Hummingbird's autopsy!

'Hey, Glen. Kirstie here.' Gripping the phone tight, trying not to rush him, she spoke calmly though she felt a surge of nervous tension. 'Matt's busy. But if it's about the autopsy report, you can tell me and I'll pass on the information.'

'Kirstie, hi. Listen, tell Matt I got his message, but not until early this morning.'

She bit her lip to control her disappointment. 'That's OK. I'll explain that the report isn't ready yet. Maybe tomorrow?'

'No, you don't understand.' The vet hesitated, then decided to continue. 'The fact is, I was away from home all day yesterday. I just flew in from

New York on the red-eye flight, so I didn't pick up any of my messages.'

'Right.' A doubt took root in Kirstie's mind and blossomed into a big fear. 'So what happened to Hummingbird after you took her away from here on Thursday?'

'I didn't do that in person,' Glen explained. 'I had one of my assistants drive out for me. That was Amy. She did what we normally do in that situation – drove the body back to the veterinary centre and disposed of the remains right away.'

Kirstie closed her eyes to grapple with the information. 'You mean we can't – it's not possible to discover why Hummingbird died?'

The vet paused again. 'I'm sorry, Kirstie. Given the blizzard and the young age of the foal, we had it down as hypothermia, no question. The corpse went straight in the incinerator. So you see, it's way, way too late.'

'Yeah, hopes get raised, then they get dashed down again,' Hadley muttered.

He'd come into the tack-room office to find Kirstie leaning on the desk and hanging her head. He'd patiently listened to her garbled explanation of how the autopsy report was meant to clear Sandy of neglect and now it couldn't because Matt hadn't put in the request on time.

'It's not fair,' she complained. 'Leon Powell doesn't know what he's talking about but he has a heap of money and friends like Ron Waterson to help him out. What chance do we stand if we don't have evidence from the autopsy?'

'It was a neat idea,' Hadley admitted, going back out on to the porch. 'But sometimes things don't work out. We gotta accept that.'

Easy to say if you're not the one in the firing line, Kirstie thought. She envisaged the attorneys' letters dropping thick and fast on the doormat once Leon Powell had got his case together. Her mom stood more or less alone against the system.

'Talk to Lisa about it,' Hadley suggested, as if he thought girl talk was what Kirstie needed.

'I can't – we're not – I mean, she's not here!' *Trust the old man to say the wrong thing*.

'Sure she is,' he contradicted. 'Her grandpa just dropped her off outside the house. She's knocking on the door right now.'

'I'm not here to say sorry and grovel!' Lisa told

Kirstie straight out. 'So if you expect me to, I'm outta here!'

'Me neither!' Kirstie replied. She stood warily by the window, keeping the kitchen table between her and Lisa.

There was a long, silent stare.

'So why come?' Kirstie challenged.

'I'll get to that. Just so long as you're not looking for me to eat dirt.' Lisa's eyes were wide, her jaw determined. She even stood with her hands on her hips to make her message clear.

'Don't push it,' Kirstie warned. She still felt sore about the way Lisa had walked out on her.

'I just couldn't handle it, OK! The blizzard, the foal dying out there. And you couldn't see that all the stuff about mystery reasons was pushing me over the edge.'

'Hmm.' Kirstie folded her arms. 'It was – it still is important.'

Lisa nodded. 'I've been thinking about it all last night and this morning and I agree with you. Not that I'm saying sorry, OK! I'm saying, yeah we need to find out exactly how Hummingbird died.'

'Hmm.' This time, Kirstie's grunt was hollow. 'We do?'

'I'm saying "we", if that's what you mean.' By this time Lisa's arms had fallen to her sides and her voice was softer. 'I would like to help on this. And I'd like us to get back to where we were – you and me.'

'Me too,' Kirstie murmured. She let out a loud sigh. 'Actually I am sorry for yelling and going on.'

Lisa gave a faint, relieved smile. 'Me too.' Her lip quivered, then she quickly stiffened it. 'Enough already! So what do we do to stop the dreaded Leon in his tracks?'

'OK, so now you're gonna give in?' was Lisa's challenge.

Over lunch, Kirstie had brought her up to date and admitted that the phone call from Glen Woodford had left her feeling hopeless. The afternoon rides had departed and the girls were standing in the sunny arena with Columbine and Skylark.

Lisa pushed harder. 'Yeah, you're gonna give in, like Skylark's giving in. You're thinking, "There's nothing I can do!"'

Connecting the two things in her mind gave Kirstie a shock. *Am I like poor Skylark?* she thought.

And has she really lost all hope as Lisa says?

One look across the arena told her that the picture as far as Skylark was concerned was as gloomy as ever. Even the bright spring sunshine and the revived hillsides, after the storm, had failed to lift her head or get her to take any apparent interest in the antics of the playful burro.

'How come yesterday you wanted to play detective and now today you don't?' Lisa quizzed.

'Yesterday I was counting on Matt and Glen Woodford to help,' Kirstie pointed out.

'Yeah? So one door closes. Is that it – *finito*?'

Kirstie sighed. 'Quit giving me the third degree. Tell me an idea instead.'

Lisa thought hard. 'OK, what do we know about Skylark's history? She hasn't been at Half-Moon Ranch long, has she?'

Though she didn't see where this would lead, Kirstie racked her brains for an answer. 'We bought her last fall. She was already in foal. Mom was told this was her first pregnancy. That's all I know.'

'You don't know who owned her or where she was sold?'

'No. But what's the big idea?'

'I'm not sure exactly? But that kind of information

108

couldn't do any harm. So how would we find out?' Still Lisa rained the questions on Kirstie, who caved in under pressure.

'Ben will have it on file,' she told her, leading the way out of the arena and into the head wrangler's office. She knew the password to access details about the ramuda on the computer and was soon clicking the mouse until she reached Skylark's name.

'It says we bought her from the sale barn in Renegade,' she said, pointing with the cursor. 'Name of previous owner is Rogers. Address – Cascade Valley Ranch, ten miles north of Renegade on the T85.'

'Gotcha!' Lisa said, jotting down the details.

'So?' Kirstie queried. Lisa's energy made her feel suddenly weary.

'So now we call the Rogers, ask for the lowdown on why they sent Skylark off to the sale barn while she was in foal,' came the answer. 'After all, doesn't it strike you as weird?'

'What's weird about it?' Kirstie asked.

Lisa gave her a pitying look, then spelled it out. 'They sell one horse in the fall. If they'd waited until spring they could've sold two, earned more dough. That's what's weird – get it?'

8

'Hi. My name's Kirstie Scott. I'd like to speak with Mr Rogers, please.' Kirstie looked at Lisa, eyes wide, voice a little shaky. This was one important phone call!

'Trace Rogers? He ain't here.' The answer was abrupt and to the point.

'That is Cascade Valley Ranch?' Kirstie checked.

'Yep. Do you want to make a reservation?'

'Well, not exactly. I need to talk to the owner.'

'That's me,' the voice replied. 'Trace Rogers sold out last fall. I'm Walt Adkins. How can I help?'

Kirstie hesitated over the news that the ranch had

a new owner. 'I wanted to ask Mr Rogers about a broodmare named Skylark—' she began.

'Jeez, what is this? Why does everyone want to know about one no-good horse all of a sudden?' Walt Adkins interrupted. 'Listen, honey, I don't know nothin' about no Skylark. I run this place without broodmares. I buy in all my stock ready broke and get them out on the trails earning dough just as soon as I can. Period. End of story.'

'But would you know where Mr Rogers is now?' Kirstie persisted.

Walt Adkins came back more impatient than ever. 'I already told you, I don't know and I don't wanna know.'

The line went dead and Kirstie put down the phone. 'Gee, thanks!' she muttered.

'For nothing!' Lisa added.

They went and hung out on the porch swing, gazing out along the valley and up to the twin summits of Eagle's Peak and Tigawon Mount.

'Huh,' Lisa murmured, kicking the swing into gentle action. They rocked to and fro. 'That sucks.'

Kirstie nodded. To and fro. The sun was sinking, shadows lengthening. In the arena Skylark had sought out the darkest corner and hung her head in misery. 'You know something?' Kirstie muttered slowly, going on gut reaction, without any hard evidence. 'Walt Adkins wasn't the genuine article.'

Lisa stopped the swing with her foot. She swivelled and stared at Kirstie. 'What are you saying?'

'He had something to hide,' Kirstie answered.

'Are you kidding?'

'Nope.' She got up and walked across the yard.

'What? I mean, why? Kirstie, wait!' Lisa ran after her.

'I don't know what and I don't know why,' she admitted. It was time to lead Skylark into her stall and bed her down for the night. 'But tomorrow I sure plan to find out.'

Saturday was the day for taking the broodmares back out to Pond Meadow, Sandy and Ben had decided.

'The snow's melted and the ground has dried out,' he'd informed her. 'It's time to get them out to grass.'

It was a job for the early morning and Kirstie and Lisa were up to help before it was properly light. While Ben drove the trailer to the barn, the girls had begun to lead out Taco and Yukon. The two paint mares and their foals had come willingly and the loading went smoothly, Snickers following on without a protest. Within minutes, all six horses were in the trailer and Ben had headed out to the far meadow.

'Without Skylark, 'Lisa noted sadly, watching the trailer disappear round the first bend in Five Mile Creek Trail.

Kirstie sighed heavily. 'What are we gonna do about her? More than two days is a long time to go without food. She's not even drinking much either.'

'When does it get serious?' Lisa asked, following Kirstie into the barn.

Kirstie arrived at Skylark's stall and prepared to lead her out into the arena. The lonely mare had watched the departure of the others and seemed to feel her isolation more keenly than ever. She stood in total dejection, her face turned away, her thin body trembling. 'It's serious now,' Kirstie replied. 'The only question is, exactly when do we call in the vet?'

Her answer made them both shiver, then rush to change the subject. As soon as they'd taken Skylark to join Moondance and Columbine, they went looking for Hadley to ask him a favour.

'Hadley, what are you doing this afternoon?' Lisa made the first smiling approach after they'd come across him polishing off a breakfast of bacon and waffles in the small bunkhouse kitchen.

The old man dunked his empty plate into a sinkful of hot, soapy water. 'There's twenty things I might be doin',' he stalled. 'Includin' a visit to my manicurist and an appointment with my hair stylist.'

'Yeah, ha-ha!' Kirstie laughed. 'No really, Hadley, would you be willing to drive us over to Renegade?'

He stopped washing his dishes and shot her a sharp look. 'What's in Renegade?'

'Gas stations, stores, a manicurist . . . !' Lisa got her own back.

But Kirstie kept on the pressure. 'We'd like to visit Cascade Valley Ranch, which is where Skylark came from originally,' she explained. 'We reckon that if we find out more about her history, there may be some other explanation of why her foal died out there in Pond Meadow.'

Hadley was quick to grasp their line of thinking. Swooshing plates through the hot water as Kirstie went into detail, he tilted his head this way and that. 'Count me in,' he told them when she'd finished.

'I'd be more than happy to pay Mr Walt Adkins a neighbourly visit.'

So that was fixed and the morning routine running smoothly when the arrival of an unexpected visitor blew all thoughts of Cascade Valley from Kirstie's and Lisa's minds.

It came in the shape of a silver Jeep driven by a middle-aged woman dressed in a practical denim shirt, fringed black leather vest and jeans. Something about her determined air as she got out of the Jeep set up alarm bells and Kirstie left off raking the yard to follow the woman into the house.

Sandy had already invited her in when Kirstie arrived. She introduced the newcomer in a strained, quiet voice. 'Kirstie, this is Suzi Valentine. She works for the Dude Ranch Association.'

Suzi offered to shake hands but there was no warmth in her smile. 'Pleased to meet you,' she said politely. 'My organisation has sent me along to check out staff training and horse management. Your mom had a letter from us earlier this week.'

Kirstie felt her throat go dry. She stammered something meaningless then backed away against the door.

'It's OK. We're happy to show Suzi around.' Sandy papered over the awkward silence. 'I'm gonna ask Karina to explain how things work, staff-wise. Then I plan to get Ben to talk about the equine side.'

Her mom didn't show any obvious sign of anxiety but Kirstie knew she was putting on an act. To Sandy, the good reputation of Half-Moon Ranch meant the whole world. It was her living, the way she kept her family together, a link with her own parents who had run the ranch before her – everything!

'This is stupid!' Kirstie blurted out. 'Just because one dumb guest comes to you with a made-up story, you come out here and put my mom under all this pressure!'

'Kirstie!' Sandy warned.

Suzi Valentine tilted her head to one side, hearing Kirstie's outburst and considering it carefully. 'I understand,' she said calmly. 'And normally we would take a little more time before we acted. But I'm afraid this isn't just some dumb guest. I'm not giving anything away when I tell you that the complainant is none other than Leon Powell. And because of who he is, he has the power to make a big noise.'

116

The visitor paused to take a newspaper out of the attaché case she carried with her. 'This is this morning's *Denver Post*,' she told them, opening up the paper and laying it on the table. She pointed to a headline and a large colour photograph.

Kirstie recognised the picture straight away. It showed Skylark and Hummingbird in Pond Meadow – the very photograph that she had a copy of. Skylark and her foal in the sunshine, with spring flowers everywhere. 'Picture by Leon Powell', it said underneath. Across the top of the page was a hard-hitting headline – 'Scandal of Neglect at Half-Moon Ranch!'

It was hard to focus on the content of the article. Kirstie felt sick in her stomach at the damage the artist had done. She read how badly trained staff frequently mistreated the horses and how newborn foals like the one in the picture were left to die in a blizzard. Powell named names – he targeted wrangler Karina Cooper for special blame and announced in an exclusive interview with the feature writer that he was launching a big legal action against ranch owner Sandy Scott.

Kirstie finished reading but couldn't speak.

'My Association has to be seen to act,' Suzi

Valentine insisted quietly. 'They sent me specifically to investigate these claims and that's what I intend to do!'

Still speechless, Kirstie watched her mom lead the visitor across the yard in search of Karina.

Crazy, mean-minded Leon Powell! Big-mouth! Stupid little guy! She cursed and called him names in a burst of helpless anger. Then she seized the newspaper and ran straight to Ron Waterson's cabin. 'Take a look at this!' she yelled when she spotted him cleaning his boots on the porch. She thrust the article under his nose. 'I suppose you encouraged your precious client to print this stuff!'

The lawyer took a step back, reached into his shirt pocket for his glasses and read the headline. 'I certainly did not,' he said stiffly, carefully replacing his glasses and frowning into the middle distance. 'As a matter of fact, I instructed Leon not to go to the media – yet!'

'Well, he sure took your advice!' Kirstie said scornfully. 'I guess that's where you were yesterday – in town with Leon, talking to journalists.'

'I don't think you heard what I just said,' Ron Waterson insisted. 'My advice, for what it was worth,

118

was not to publish accusations until I'd completed some groundwork on the case.'

As Kirstie fumed and roughly folded the newspaper, she heard Lisa running to join them.

Lisa arrived breathless and flustered. 'Kirstie, did you know the woman in the Jeep is here to investigate you?'

'I know it. Say, we're having a great day and we haven't got beyond breakfast!' Lurching from anger to hopelessness, Kirstie handed Lisa the paper. 'Y'know something? Why don't we call off our trip to Cascade Valley? I mean, really, what good is it gonna do?'

Ron Waterson, who had calmly carried on cleaning his boots, stopped at this point and made no secret of the fact that he was paying full attention to Kirstie and Lisa's conversation.

'Would you stop blowing hot and cold on me!' Lisa retorted. 'Either we figure it's worth trying to unearth some other reason why Hummingbird might have died or we don't!'

'Hush!' Realising that they could be overheard, Kirstie drew Lisa to one side. 'What's the betting he picks up the phone and tells his buddy, Leon, our latest plan?'

Lisa gulped. 'Sorry, I didn't think.' Making a zipper signal across her lips, Lisa looked over her shoulder. 'It's OK, he's going into his cabin. We can relax.'

'Too late,' Kirstie sighed. 'Anyhow, it was my fault. I blew my top big time, and I was the one who mentioned the name of the ranch. Now the other side is on to it, they're bound to follow it up.'

'Yeah, but what can they do?' Lisa led the way down to the corral, where guests were gathering for the morning ride.

'They can contact Walt Adkins for starters,' Kirstie pointed out. 'They can pay him not to talk to us. They can also use him to track down Trace Rogers.'

Lisa thought about this in silence. 'You're sure we're not paranoid? I mean, that's like paying off witnesses – it would be bribery!'

Kirstie nodded. 'I know. But look at what Powell has already done to us. Why should he stop there, especially if he finds out that Trace Rogers has some information that could be useful to Mom?'

Convinced, Lisa came up with the suggestion that the best thing she and Kirstie could do would be to move the planned visit to Renegade forward to the morning. 'That's if Hadley is free,' she added, running off to the bunkhouse to find him.

This left Kirstie to pace along the corral fence, paying little attention to the activity inside. As usual, Ben had split the groups and described the planned routes while Sandy and Matt checked cinches and helped guests on to their horses. Karina, who would normally be there working, was talking earnestly with Suzi Valentine at the entrance to the barn.

Drawn to where they stood, Kirstie slipped through the gate and sloped quietly across.

'And exactly how long have you been working with horses, Ms Cooper?' Suzi was saying in that annoyingly calm, patronising way.

Karina had a steely, stubborn look in her eye. 'I bin brush poppin' cattle since I was ten years old,' she drawled.

'Brush popping cattle?' echoed a mystified investigator.

'I was a buckaroo up in Idaho, then I worked eight years gentlin' horses for Tex Gunnersen, who runs the best outfit south of Durango. Any more questions?' Karina said.

'Buckaroo . . . gentling . . .' Slowly Suzi jotted down the answer in her notebook. 'Now, about this incident with the young horse, out on Bear Hunt Overlook. Could you describe to me in detail the method you employed to control her?'

Kirstie saw Karina roll her eyes heavenwards. *Don't lose it this time!* she prayed silently, though she knew she had no room to talk. *Cool it Karina, for heaven's sakes!*

The wrangler was gathering herself for her reply when Kirstie spotted Lisa and Hadley emerge from the bunkhouse and walk towards the corral. At the same time, Ron Waterson was hurrying down from his cabin, evidently late for his ride.

'C'mon, Kirstie!' Lisa hailed her. 'Hadley's dropped everything for us. We can go right away!'

Kirstie groaned when she saw that the lawyer had overheard once more. Then she ran quickly to stop Lisa giving away more. 'Let's go!' she gabbled, only stopping to grab her hat from the place where she'd left it on the gatepost. She dodged past Ron Waterson's tall figure and ran on towards Hadley's pick-up.

But Waterson turned and followed her. She could hear his footsteps crunching over the dirt; she saw Lisa and Hadley stop and cast puzzled looks then brace themselves for an argument. So Kirstie stopped, turned and challenged him. 'What do you want?' she demanded.

'I want to talk to you,' he replied, expressionless as ever.

'We have nothing to say!' If a face-off was what Waterson wanted, Kirstie was ready. 'This is a free country. We can go where we want, do as we like!'

The lawyer gave one of his remote stares. Evidently deciding that it was better to deal with Hadley than a hot-headed kid, he brushed past. 'I wouldn't advise driving out to Renegade,' he began.

'You wouldn't, huh?' The old wrangler took in the facts that Sandy had left the corral and was heading their way, plus Karina and Suzi Valentine were following fast on her heels. It seemed that they were set up for a full-scale confrontation and Hadley was never one to back down. 'Well, mister, we're not about to take that advice.'

Waterson showed a flicker of irritation – the first emotion that Kirstie had ever spotted on his thin, serious face. 'You don't understand,' he snapped.

'Sure we do.' Hadley squared his shoulders. 'It ain't difficult. You work for Powell. Powell is tryin' to destroy this ranch. We won't hang around and let you do that. Period!'

Yes! Kirstie felt defiance surge through her. She didn't care that her mom looked troubled or that the official from the Dude Ranch Association was poised to take down notes. *Way to go, Hadley!* she urged silently. *Give this guy a real hard time!*

The lawyer's frown deepened. 'Believe me, a visit to Cascade Valley would be a waste of your time.'

'Don't listen to him, Hadley,' Lisa insisted, ready to open the pick-up door. 'Let's go.'

Ron Waterson shook his head. He turned to Sandy in an appeal for common sense. 'Are you going to hear me out?' he demanded.

She nodded briefly. 'Go ahead.'

'OK. A visit to Walt Adkins will not produce any further information.' Waterson was clear and calm again. 'The reason is, I've already spoken to him. I had my driver take me there yesterday. I gathered all the evidence I need.'

9

Kirstie thought Hadley was going to walk up to Waterson and punch him. She saw Lisa's face turn red with anger and her mom close her eyes in defeat.

Powell and his lawyer had the whole thing sewn up.

'How much did you pay Adkins not to talk to us?' Kirstie demanded. She recalled the ranch owner's vagueness when they'd spoken on the phone. And he'd made that weird remark about everyone getting interested in Skylark all of a sudden. Of course, now it was crystal clear that he'd already had the visit from Ron Waterson.

The lawyer raised his eyebrows. 'You think I bribed Adkins?'

'Sure you did!' Lisa insisted. 'This whole thing stinks!'

As Sandy moved forward to intervene and Suzi Valentine took in every detail, Ron Waterson raised both hands and spoke heatedly. 'Hold it! Would everyone just listen to me for a darned second!'

The change in him startled them into silence. *What happened to the cool, calm, collected lawyer?* Kirstie wondered.

'OK, are you ready? Let's introduce some hard facts here. Yes, I did visit Cascade Valley. No, it wasn't under instructions from Leon Powell. I went because I needed to clear up a few things in my own mind.'

'Stop!' Still suspicious, Kirstie came in with another challenge. 'How come you knew we bought Skylark from Cascade Valley? Did you hack into our computer records?'

Ron Waterson gave a short, dry laugh. 'Good thinking. But no, I didn't need to do that. The fact is, I was a guest at Cascade Valley in September last year. I saw the bay mare there with my own eyes.'

'You did?' Kirstie was stunned.

'Yeah. And I wasn't impressed by the outfit, I must admit. In fact, I left three days early. Then the minute I walked into this mess and saw Skylark, I thought I remembered her from last fall. But I needed to drive out and speak with Trace Rogers before I made any moves.'

This was getting really weird. Looking round, Kirstie saw the puzzled frowns. Where was Powell's lawyer leading them? Was this a clever trick? Or did he have something new to tell them?

'Trace Rogers left Cascade Valley,' she pointed out. 'Is that the reason you're telling us that our trip out there would be a waste of time?'

'Good thinking again,' Waterson conceded. 'But wrong a second time. What I discovered yesterday was that Rogers sold out to his cousin, Walt Adkins, due to financial problems. However, Rogers didn't leave. He stayed on and now works for Adkins in the capacity of head wrangler.'

'So you were able to talk to Rogers after all!'

Ron Waterson nodded. 'It wasn't easy, let me tell you. My guess is that neither of those two cousins is comfortable talking to lawyers or having outsiders pry into their business. Anyhow, let's say my persistence paid off. In the end, Adkins produced his head wrangler to talk to me on the subject of the bay broodmare.'

Kirstie held her breath and took another look around. At this point, nobody else seemed about to interrupt Ron Waterson's fascinating account. 'Did you ask him why he sold Skylark when she was in foal?' she asked in a voice not much above a whisper.

Waterson nodded. 'You'll like the answer, I think.'

'So?' Kirstie felt her fingernails digging into her palms as the tension of the moment got to her.

'Rogers told me, under pressure, that he got rid of the mare because she produced unreliable foals.'

'Now wait a minute!' Sandy stepped forward. 'In the record Rogers sent to the sale barn, he stated that Skylark was a first time broodmare – in effect, this was her first pregnancy.'

'Yes but it turns out he falsified the file because he knew her value would take a dive if he admitted the truth.'

'Which is what?' Sandy asked quietly.

Waterson answered simply. 'That Skylark had already produced two foals. One was stillborn. The other died when it was four weeks old.'

* * *

Ron Waterson's shock announcement opened the floodgates for questions, led by Hadley, the real horse expert amongst them.

'What was the official verdict on the mare's poor record?' he wanted to know. 'Did Rogers get a vet in?'

Waterson nodded. 'Eventually. They diagnosed a rare genetic disorder – something that Skylark inherited and passes on to her foals. Her offspring are born with a cardiovascular disease which means that their hearts are weak and consequently their chances of survival beyond a month or two are practically nil.'

'So Hummingbird was bound to die?' Lisa sighed.

Kirstie recalled a memory of the tiny foal trying out her long, skinny legs and skipping to keep up with her mom in the sunny meadow. No sign then of the shadow hanging over her. And, with a sharp regret, she remembered Skylark's motherly pride.

'I'm afraid so,' the lawyer confirmed.

'So the foal didn't freeze to death?' Suzi Valentine asked. She'd begun to loosen up and offer Sandy a smile of encouragement.

'Probably not. Though we can never be one hundred per cent sure.'

'But it knocks a hole right through Leon Powell's claims of neglect,' Hadley insisted.

Another memory – a slow-motion picture that recalled for Kirstie the moment when she entered the draw in the blizzard. She saw again Skylark bravely standing guard over Hummingbird. A layer of snow covered the foal like a funeral shroud. The mare turned her head and her eyes were hopeless. Three foals, all of them dead.

'So how come you're offering us all this fresh information?' Hadley wanted to know. 'Shouldn't you be quietly feeding it to Powell and awaiting your client's instructions or whatever it is that you lawyers do?'

Ron Waterson paused. '*Ex*-client,' he corrected. 'And *ex*-friend. When I saw what he'd given to this morning's newspaper, I called him and gave it to him straight. I guess I said he was a jumped-up, egotistical, third-rate phoney.'

Lisa gasped and let her mouth fall open. 'You did!'

Ron nodded. 'I did more than that. I told him that there was absolutely no case against Half-Moon Ranch, that he'd gone ahead and made a total ass of himself and, what's more, I quit!'

* * *

'How about that!' Lisa murmured for the twentieth time at least as she and Kirstie mucked out Skylark's stall that lunchtime.

'Yeah,' Kirstie agreed. 'Here we were picturing Ron as part of the Evil Force out to destroy us yet all along he was quietly working his way towards the truth.'

'And thanks to him your mom can relax.' Lisa scattered fresh straw and fluffed it up for Skylark's comfort when they brought her in from the corral. 'Leon Powell is in deep trouble for printing a lie and it's his good name that's gonna take a dive, not yours. Plus, the Dude Ranch lady gave you the all-clear.'

'All because of Ron!' Kirstie shook her head over it. 'Y'know what they say – never judge a book . . .'

'I know. He looks so stiff and unfriendly yet underneath he's a teddy bear. Did you see his face when your mom hugged him and thanked him. He turned cherry red and didn't know where to look but you could tell he was happy that it had worked out for everyone.'

'Except for Skylark,' Kirstie pointed out.' It didn't work out for her exactly. 'How mean was it of Rogers

131

to breed her a third time, knowing what he did about the two previous foals!'

'Not to mention selling the horse to you with false records. Anyhow, Ron says he plans to prosecute them over that. And he also asked Suzi Valentine to move in on their spread to check them out. With luck that should improve standards at Cascade Valley long term.'

Kirstie had been pleased by this when she'd first heard it but now she wanted to concentrate on Skylark and the one question that still hung over them. 'C'mon, Matt!' she muttered, striding to the door to look out across the corral. 'How can eating lunch take him twenty whole minutes?'

Carrying a headcollar, Lisa slid by. 'Let's fetch Skylark in from the arena while we're waiting,' she suggested.

They'd done this, having a word with Moondance and Columbine on the way, and were putting Skylark into her stall when Matt showed up at last.

'Yeah, yeah, I'm late,' he acknowledged. 'But I had to stop and look up this genetic problem in my college textbook. Luckily, Ron had made a note of the exact Latin name so I've been able to read up about it.'

'And is it possible that the broodmare who passes it down the line can develop the same condition?' Kirstie asked anxiously.

This was the big question that had occurred to her as soon as Ron Waterson had broken his news to them. Might Skylark be sick with a weak heart too?

There'd been no one around to answer it. Hadley and Karina had both shaken their heads and said it was a vet thing. Sandy had suggested they ask Matt when he came back from his trail-ride.

So here they were now, watching him take a stethoscope and a syringe kit from his bag.

'Matt, did the book say that the mother could be sick as well?' Kirstie insisted.

He nodded without looking at her. 'Fifty-fifty chance,' he admitted.

Kirstie took a deep breath. She held on to Skylark's lead-rope as Matt began to examine her, even though the mare showed no signs of resisting. Instead, she waited listless as ever as the stethoscope was placed against her chest and sides.

'So?' Lisa asked.

Matt stood up straight and unhooked the stethoscope from his ears. 'Her heart sounds OK,'

he said cautiously. Then he went to work with the syringe. 'I need to take a blood sample and send it off to Glen's lab for analysis before we can be sure,' he explained.

'But it's looking good?' Kirstie put on pressure. She hoped with all her heart to get a yes.

'In terms of having the disease herself, yes,' he conceded.

Kirstie sighed. *Thank heavens!*

'But?' Lisa prompted. 'Did you pick up something you didn't like anyway?'

Matt nodded, then continued his examination.

'Her general condition is poor. Her coat is dull, see, and her eyes and mouth are in bad shape. And those are just the external signs. When we get the blood test results back tomorrow, I'm fully expecting to find signs that her internal organs are beginning to shut down too.'

'Because she won't eat?' Lisa looked at Kirstie, who hung her head and avoided her gaze.

Another nod came from Matt. He put away his instruments and clicked shut the catch on his bag. 'We need something to happen that's gonna turn her round and make her want to live again,' he muttered.' And for the life of me I can't figure out what that might be!'

How did anyone find a solution to a problem like this, Kirstie wondered. She felt the seriousness of Matt's reply weigh her down as she led Skylark slowly towards the arena, leaving Lisa to clean out the uneaten grain from the manger and replace it with fresh hay.

You couldn't just say, 'Live!' and expect Skylark to forget her lost foals. You couldn't say 'Eat!' and force the food down her throat. An animal had a strong will to survive but when the spirit was broken, there was no human skill or scrap of knowledge in the world that could mend it again.

So Kirstie's heart was heavy in the full force of the midday sun. She felt Skylark drag her feet unwillingly, refusing to look up even when Karina swung open the arena gate and emerged riding an excited Moondance.

'Jeez, I'm late for the afternoon ride!' Karina exclaimed, thanking Kirstie as she stood to one side. 'Ben's gonna have my hide!'

Kirstie watched the smooth action of Hadley's blue roan mare as she broke into a trot. Karina's seat was as tight and upright as could be, her legs long in the stirrups, hands easy on the reins.

That's how life should be for a young horse, Kirstie thought – *joyful, eager, wanting to be out there*.

Not that Columbine agreed with her. The little burro obviously wanted her companion back in the arena with her, to judge by the angry *ee-aws*. Wow, was that an ugly sound!

Kirstie winced as she led Skylark through the gate. But then she smiled when she saw what Columbine was doing. Somehow she'd tipped over the plastic manger and jumped on top of it. She was perched there, head back, eyes closed, braying for all she was worth. *Come back, Moondance! What about me!*

The sight brought a brief smile to Kirstie's face as she released Skylark from the headcollar. 'You're a cutie,' she murmured, approaching the burro and offering to scratch her hairy back. 'But you're a noisy little crittur. How about cutting out the *ee-aws* and giving us some peace?'

Eee-aaawww! Columbine screeched. She jumped down from the upturned manger and crow-hopped her way across the dusty enclosure, kicking up her heels like a tiny bucking bronc. Reaching the fence, she slid to a halt, turned and began the whole thing over, ending at the gate with another 'Take me with you!' bray.

Kirstie smiled again. Then her attention was distracted by a shout from Lisa, standing in the doorway to the barn and holding up what looked like a two-way radio.

'Hey, Kirstie, look what I found!' Lisa yelled.

Eee-aaww! Columbine drowned out the rest.

Kirstie took the most direct way to escape from the burro's racket, running across the arena to vault over the fence and into the empty corral. Then she jogged easily towards the barn. 'Whose is the radio?' she called back.

'I told you already – it looks like Karina's.' Lisa showed her the handwritten label stuck to the side. 'Isn't she gonna need it this afternoon?'

'She sure is,' Kirstie replied. 'I guess she was in such a hurry she forgot it. C'mon, let's use the transmitter in Ben's office to call him and let him know the situation.'

'Will he want us to saddle up and ride out after Karina's group?' Lisa asked hopefully. 'We could soon catch up and hand over the radio.'

'Maybe.' Entering the dark tack-room, Kirstie made her way into the back office. Soon she was talking to the head wrangler and seeking his advice.

'If Hadley's around, get him to drive the pick-up along Miners' Ridge to Dead Man's Canyon,' he told her, dashing Lisa's hopes. 'That's the quickest way to hook up with Karina's group. Over.'

'Gotcha. Over.' Kirstie flicked off the radio and shrugged at Lisa. 'Hey, you win some, you lose some.'

She was out in the sunshine, heading up the slope to Hadley's cabin, when something odd struck her. *It's awful quiet!* she said to herself, turning quickly to look back down at the arena.

She gasped sharply. The gate had swung open.

She could see Skylark standing passively in the shadow of the tack-room. But searching the whole area – once, then twice so as to be absolutely sure – she could see no sign of the noisy burro.

10

'Oh, great!' Lisa spotted the empty arena at the same time as Kirstie. 'The case of the vanishing burro!'

Kirstie ran back to close the gate. 'How stupid can I be?' she groaned. 'Leaving a gate open is the dumbest thing!'

Skylark looked up at them, then dropped her head and turned away.

'Don't beat yourself up. It's easy to do and Columbine can't be far away,' Lisa said, scanning the yard and the corral. 'I mean, how far can she travel out there all alone?'

'As far as Eagle's Peak if she takes it into her head.' Kirstie's reply was only half joking. 'Listen, I'll run and hand Karina's radio over to Hadley like we planned. You take a look inside the barn, see if Columbine snuck in there to find extra food.'

'OK, but make it fast!' Beginning to realise that tracking down the sneaky little burro might not be easy, Lisa turned serious.

So Kirstie accomplished her errand and ran back, hoping that by now Lisa would have caught Columbine with her nose in the grain barrel, eating herself stupid. That's what any sane escapee donkey would have done.

'Nope!' Lisa emerged from the barn shaking her head. 'Not a sign. Did you tell Hadley?'

'Yeah. He says he'll keep a lookout for her as he drives out to Miners' Ridge. Or, to use his exact words – "That squirly crittur ain't got a lick of cow sense. Best git her back before she scatters to hell!" '

'OK!' Lisa organised her thoughts. 'Looking back to the moment when she broke free, what was she doing right then?'

'Letting Moondance know that she didn't like being left behind. Hey, do you figure Columbine lit out after her buddy?' Immediately Kirstie set about examining the sets of prints that headed out along Meltwater Trail, hoping to see the little donkey's tiny hooves amongst the metal shod horses'.

Lisa left it to the expert, hovering on the grass verge. 'Any luck?'

'Maybe.' But the prints outside the corral were so scuffed and jumbled that Kirstie couldn't be sure. She shook her head and sighed, picturing the scatty burro making her dash for open country. 'You'd think we'd hear her bray.'

Seeing Hadley drive by in his pick-up, Lisa gave him a thumbs-down sign to show that as yet they'd had no luck. 'Listen, since Hadley is checking Karina and Moondance's route, maybe we should try some place else.'

Kirstie racked her brains to work out an alternative. But when it came down to it, all she could suggest was that they start the search close to the ranch and gradually and systematically spiral outwards.

'Big ranch, small burro,' was Lisa's gloomy reply.

But they had to begin somewhere – on foot at first, then taking Lucky and Rodeo Rocky out of Red Fox Meadow and riding them on the beginner trails closest to home.

'Eighteen mule deer, one coyote, five black squirrels and a chipmunk!' Lisa listed the wildlife they'd spotted by three in the afternoon. 'Zero burros!'

Kirstie was hot and worried. They'd searched the fringe of forest at the back of Red Fox Meadow, then come down into the valley without a single sighting of Columbine. They'd criss-crossed the creek, weaving in and out of bright green willows, then ridden up the south slopes towards Angel Rock. Now they let Lucky and Rocky rest in the shade of more ponderosa pines.

She looked at her watch. In less than an hour the afternoon rides would be returning and she would have to confess her careless blunder to her mom. Meanwhile, the runaway burro would be out here all alone, with evening drawing in and coyotes on the prowl.

'What now?' Lisa asked, easing her feet back into the stirrups. She rolled up her shirt-sleeves and fanned her hot face.

'We keep looking,' Kirstie sighed.

As Lisa herself had said – big ranch, small burro.

* * *

Two hours later and still empty handed, the girls reluctantly turned their horses for home.

'I guess Hadley will have told Mom what happened,' Kirstie murmured as they came within sight of the red barn roofs. 'Jeez, I'm gonna be in big trouble.'

'I'll say it wasn't your fault,' Lisa offered.

'Thanks, but it was.' Kirstie trotted Lucky round the back way behind the barn, hoping to keep out of Sandy's way for the time being. 'It was totally down to me.'

They were silent as they slunk into the corral.

'Hey, Kirstie.' Ben approached with a casual greeting. 'I hear you let the burro escape!'

'Yeah, yeah! We've been looking for her all afternoon.' Sheepishly she slid from the saddle and tethered Lucky to the rail.

'No big deal,' Ben assured her. 'Your mom and Karina rode out to take a look. We'll find her before dusk, no problem.'

'Wasn't Mom mad at me?'

'Nope. You're the golden girl who brought back seven horses in the snow, remember. Besides, a burro is like a pony – come feed time, she finds her way home, no problem. Speaking of which, will you two girls bring Skylark in from the arena and try to get her to eat supper for a change.'

They nodded and slipped away. Finding the bay mare in her dark corner, Kirstie went to fetch her.

Skylark's back was turned as usual. But straight away Kirstie noticed a difference in her attitude. For a start, her head was up and she seemed to be listening to a sound in the distance. Then, before Kirstie had time to attach the lead-rope, she turned and walked impatiently towards the gate.

Kirstie was taken aback. *What happened to the dejected sigh, the lethargic, hanging head?* She almost had to run to catch up.

'Don't tell me you're hungry at last!' Lisa too was surprised. She let Skylark pass through the gate. 'This is cool!' she hissed, expecting the sick mare to make a beeline for the barn.

Instead, Skylark swerved wide of the corral. She paused, turned her head towards Kirstie and Lisa, flicked her ears, then walked on.

'She's heading for Five Mile Creek Trail!' Kirstie muttered.

'What got into her?' Lisa chased after Skylark, who kept just ahead. 'Isn't she supposed to be seriously sick?'

Kirstie nodded. 'But look, she's letting us know this is important!'

Once more Skylark stopped. She pawed the ground with her front hoof and snorted for them to follow. Her head was up, her ears pointing forward to pick up the sounds that only she could hear.

'It's Columbine!' Suddenly Kirstie understood. 'Lisa, we're so dumb!'

'Why? What happened?'

Skylark set off again, forcing her weak frame into a rough trot and sticking close to the creek. It was obviously an effort but one that she was determined to make.

'Don't you see?' Kirstie dragged Lisa over the rough, boggy ground. 'Skylark was there when Columbine made her getaway. She must've seen where she was headed!'

'Right!' Stumbling, then regaining her balance and picking up speed as Skylark disappeared round a sharp bend in the fast-flowing creek, Lisa got the point. 'She knew all along!'

'You see how stupid we are?' Kirstie began to sprint. 'Only, I figured Skylark was too sick to pay any attention to Columbine . . . which she is . . . so this means . . . she knows the burro can't make it home for supper . . . she's in big trouble!'

'Quit talking, save your breath,' Lisa gasped.

They rounded the bend and saw Pond Meadow spread out before them. Skylark was trotting towards the broodmares and their foals, stepping into the shallows of the stream and making progress along the pebble bed. She was breathing hard, but her head was up and every muscle tense and alert.

'I still don't see Columbine!' Kirstie followed Skylark's example of using the bed of the creek to hasten their progress. Cold water flooded into her boots but the smooth pebbles were firmer underfoot than the marshy bank.

Lisa surveyed the broad green valley. 'Me neither.'

By now the three mares had seen them. They raised their heads and whinnied, sending high, shrill cries of recognition to Skylark. The foals danced and skipped to the edge of the creek.

Thin sides heaving, Skylark stopped to return the call. Then she neighed again in a different, more urgent tone.

'That one's for Columbine!' Kirstie whispered, praying for a reply.

None came. It struck her that this was the first time Skylark had seen the meadow since her foal had died and she wondered if horses, like humans, felt the loss afresh. How hard was it for the mare to come back here? Did she hurt when she saw the healthy foals playing by the water?

If so, Skylark didn't let it push her off-course. She called again and surged on through the shallow water, running on past the foals and round another bend. Beyond this, the meadow ended and the rocks rose steeply to either side of the creek. White water formed in the narrow channel and swept round rocks at high speed.

'She'll have to climb out on to the bank soon,' Kirstie predicted. 'And so will we!'

They almost left it too late to scramble out of the creek. Lisa cried out as the current suddenly took hold of her legs and nearly swept her off her feet. Just in time, she grabbed the root of a pine tree and hauled herself on to dry land.

'It's the snowmelt!' Kirstie shouted above the sudden roar of water. She'd already checked to make sure that Skylark had come out of the creek. 'There's so much water running down from the mountains, it's like the rapids in the Canadian Rockies!'

Shivering, Lisa lifted her foot to empty out her boot while Kirstie went ahead to join Skylark. 'Take it easy!' she whispered in the horse's ear, hearing the rasp of raw breath in her throat and seeing the sweating, heaving sides. Her creamy brown coat was stained dark with water, her mane dripping.

Skylark stared ahead, brown eyes focussed on the foaming stretch of water. She called again, long and loud.

This time Kirstie heard a faint reply. Once, twice – a feeble, terrified bray.

The mare broke free, picking a way through the boulders, at times stepping into pools of swirling white water which splashed against her trembling legs and foamed high as her shoulders.

Kirstie's heart thumped. This was dangerous, crazy stuff. But if Skylark could do it so could she. She scrambled along, looking all the time for Columbine, often losing her balance and plunging sideways into the creek.

Until at last she saw the burro.

Somehow, God knows when, Columbine must have fallen into the creek. She'd been swept off her feet and floated like a log downstream until she'd come to this stretch of raging water. Maybe it had closed over her head, dragged her down and shot her back up, whirled her along, almost crushed her until it had finally dumped her on a rock, in the middle of the rapids, stranded, helpless!

A tiny abandoned creature with a big voice, crying for help.

And Skylark had heard her. Far away, from the safety of the arena, she'd picked up the sound of the burro in distress. She'd roused herself from the sorrow and misery of losing Hummingbird, responded to the forlorn cry and at last succeeded in bringing help.

Columbine teetered on the edge of the rock in the middle of the creek. For a heart stopping moment Kirstie imagined that the little donkey was about to throw herself into the wild current. 'No!' she cried, feeling Lisa come up alongside her. Rapidly she judged the distance to the rock, tried to guess how deep the water was, how fast it ran between its rocky banks.

The donkey dipped her head towards the water, then lifted it and cried.

Impatient at the delay now that she'd led the girls

to the place, Skylark snorted. She took a step into the creek to test its depth, turned, tossed her head, stepped again.

'Kirstie, we're gonna lose them both if we're not careful!' Lisa cried.

But Kirstie decided to trust Skylark. Sure, there was danger. The force of this current could sweep a strong horse to its death, never mind one weakened by hunger and grief. But Skylark's instinct for survival was roused again – she wouldn't willingly sacrifice herself. No, the mare was determined to save the burro and was working out a safe way to get to her.

So without discussing it with Lisa, Kirstie waded after Skylark and slid on to her back. She felt the pull of the water, the splash of the foam. 'Easy!' she whispered, clinging on to the horse's wet mane.

Skylark edged forward, deeper into the swollen creek.

Slowly, inch by inch, she tested the hidden bed of rocks while Columbine balanced precariously on the edge of the boulder and Kirstie leaned forward with her arms looped around the horse's neck. 'You can make it!' she whispered. Peering through the spray, she saw they were only a few feet away.

'Try to reach out!' Lisa yelled from the bank.

Were they near enough? Could Skylark stand firm and steady against the rush of water? Kirstie eased herself upright and leaned sideways, arms outstretched.

It still looked like a wide gap between her and Columbine. She could hear the donkey's feeble cry, see her terrified eyes.

'Now!' Lisa cried, seeing Skylark beginning to lose her struggle against the current. 'Tell Columbine to jump!'

Her frantic voice tipped the burro into action. She saw Kirstie's outstretched arms, leaned back on her haunches and leaped.

Kirstie took her weight, twisted her torso and sat back hard so that Skylark's body could absorb the shock of the landing. The mare staggered slightly, then recovered.

'Good girl!' Kirstie breathed. She clasped Columbine in her arms, felt Skylark turn and begin to wade slowly back towards the bank.

Now they would make it, Kirstie knew. The rapids wouldn't claim them. Skylark had beaten nature at last.

* * *

'Son of a gun!' Hadley whistled in disbelief. 'Would you look at that!'

The old wrangler was part of a crowd leaning against the arena fence. He stood between Karina and Sandy, calling to Matt and Ron Waterson to join them.

Inside the arena, Kirstie and Lisa tossed alfalfa into the manger while Skylark kept Columbine at bay.

Don't be greedy! The mare nudged the burro with her nose and when that didn't work, she lowered her head and butted her gently with her forehead.

Columbine bared her teeth and gave Skylark some downright cheek.

'Don't you let her get away with that!' Kirstie laughed. 'You teach her some manners, you hear!'

Skylark gave the youngster a stronger butt, then pushed her way forward to begin munching the hay – her first meal in three days.

'I see she found her appetite!' Ron Waterson's tall figure appeared at the fence.

'It was the swimming that did it!' Lisa called, then went on to describe Skylark's evening exercise.

Kirstie stayed a while with Skylark and Columbine. She watched the mare allow the sassy burro some space at the manger, saw her nudge and nibble the bothersome youngster like any mother would her foal. *Like she used to do with Hummingbird*, Kirstie sighed.

But that was then and this was now. Now it was Skylark and Columbine, bickering like mother and daughter.

'Would you look at that!' Hadley said again as the burro hassled the mare and the mare buffeted her away from the manger.

Columbine retreated, stopped, zigzagged crazily across the arena, then went back for more.

'A satisfactory solution,' Ron commented as Kirstie made her way to join Lisa. 'Matt here is convinced that this bonding stuff is gonna be the saving of the mare's health.'

Kirstie smiled at her brother. 'That's what I figured too!'

'I have to leave, worse luck, so I won't be here to see it with my own eyes.' Ron explained that his work was taking him home early. 'But you be sure to e-mail me about Skylark,' he told Kirstie. 'And tell me how the unusual adoption situation is coming along!'

Happily she promised to keep in touch.

'Hey and I like the way you think,' Ron continued. 'You're a smart kid. If you ever need a job some day, you come and look me up at my law firm, OK?'

Kirstie grinned. 'Thanks,' she told him, glancing over her shoulder at Skylark. The mare's coat caught the evening sun and shone reddish gold. She cast a long, graceful shadow across the white dirt. 'But the Law doesn't do it for me. It's horses with me and always will be!'